The Ballad of Tubs Marshfield

ALSO BY CARA HOFFMAN:

Bernard Pepperlin

The Ballad of Tubs Marshfield

CARA HOFFMAN

HARPER

An Imprint of HarperCollinsPublishers

ISBN 978-0-06-286547-2

Illustrations by Olivia Chin Mueller

Typography by Corina Lupp

20 21 22 23 24   CPIG   10 9 8 7 6 5 4 3 2 1

First Edition

For My Parents

The Ballad of Tubs Marshfield

PART ONE

Songs for a
Vanishing Swamp

1

Tubs was the brightest, the greenest; a frog among frogs ready to burst into song. He sported a gold-and-crimson vest and smiled like he had just heard a joke. Tubs could be counted on. His eyes were the color of the sun setting over the water, and he could swim from day to night and back again.

Tubs made his home in the roots of an old mangrove tree. Cattails grew wild in the shallow water by the porch where his boat was moored. On windy days he would watch them dancing, their long slender bodies

bowing over the marsh, all of them humming the same tune. Spider lily and trumpet vines climbed the walls of his house, the scent of their flowers drifting through the swamp like a distant melody.

The swamp was so serene, few ever ventured into the wider world. Even the birds, who could fly great distances, stayed put. Everything they needed was right there.

The roof of Tubs's house was open to let in the wind, sun, and stars. Inside, the walls were lined with jars of dried bluebottle flies and bright red rose-mallow wine, which he served on special occasions. Tubs's trombone, washboard, jaw harp, and clarinet lay out in the living room, ready to use. His piano—which was missing quite a few keys—grinned out from beneath a pile of papers, pots and pans, and fishing poles. Above his kitchen sink, Tubs had hung a portrait of his aunt Elodie, rest her soul, who had traveled as far as New

Orleans and was known for having the most beautiful voice in all the swamp.

Life was a song for Tubs. During the day, he hopped among the reeds and saw grass, or put on high rubber boots and went fishing, sitting on the bank with the dragonflies and snapping turtles. Sometimes he cooled in the dark water, sheltered by tall cypresses and the lush leaves of the mangrove trees. At midday, you could find him drifting, just beneath the surface of the swamp, his gold eyes gazing toward the hot blue heaven of the Louisiana sky.

But nothing compared to life when the sun went down and the music of the night rose up all around. The song of the water and the stones, the song of the cicadas and the leaves, the song of the ground and the paws, the howl of the fox and the wind. The near silence of the moths and the rabbits; a symphony of rustling and pauses of fluttering and digging. The birds singing their warbled questions to the night, the fish's bright splash like a faint cymbal crash. And down in the hollows of the mangroves—in the houses of the frogs—a night of reeling and song that would last until dawn. Frogs in their boats, frogs on their porches, frogs in the mud, and in the branches of trees—and Tubs at the center of it all—his house open to the world.

Tubs loved the swamp at night. Especially the summer he still had a tail and Aunt Elodie wore her crown of lightning bugs and the mud and reeds smelled wonderful and little fires blazed over the water in the distance.

Elodie had a daughter named Lila, who was Tubs's favorite cousin—and the two did everything together. When they were small, they would jump off the dock, pretending they could fly. They swam in the cool water and trekked through the forest of cattails. They fished near the garden of lily pads and talked to the water rats and ducks. While Tubs made up songs and dances and learned how to play just about any instrument, Lila read books. She liked to tell people things they didn't know and fix things that were broken.

In the evening they would talk to the swallows who came out to play as the last rays of sun shimmered over the surface of the swamp. At night they would lie in the red-and-white boat together looking up at the stars, eating mayflies and falling asleep to the high sweet sound and to the low bass drawl of their aunts and uncles, cousins and great-uncles, parents, step-parents, and godparents, nieces and nephews, brothers and sisters. Dozens of generations of frogs all living in the same place, spotted and speckled, green and yellow and mottled brown, large and small.

"Just look at that moon!" said Tubs one evening in early June. "How can anyone keep quiet when it's shining so silver?"

"The song they're singing now," Lila told him, "is two hundred and sixty-five MILLION years old." She poked him and he grinned. "Did you hear me? It's the first song our ancestors made up."

Tubs listened for a minute. Two hundred and sixty-five million years was a long time to be singing the same song. It made him want to go get his clarinet and make up something new.

"You can't make up something new," Lila said. "Every bit of water on Earth is the same water that was here to begin with. And we're all made of the creatures who came before us, and microscopic beings inhabit every inch of us."

"Huh?" said Tubs.

Lila said, "It's hard to improve on 'Kiss Me, I'm the Fattest.' If there was a better song, someone would have written it by now. Anyway," Lila said, "look at this." She pulled a letter from her pocket and handed it to

Tubs. "I haven't shown anyone yet." It was postmarked with a fancy blue-and-yellow seal—an image of a hand reaching out of the sky, holding a book.

Tubs unfolded the letter and read. It made his skin feel dry. It was from a place called the Sorbonne, which as far as he could tell was not in Louisiana. He looked up at Lila. "Where is this place?"

"In Paris," she said. "It's a school."

"Where's Paris?"

"It's across a big salt pond."

At first Tubs thought he might cry—thinking about Lila leaving was awful. But then he looked at the letter again and his heart soared for his cousin's good news. "Lila!" Tubs shouted, jumping to his feet. "Lila! This is amazing! Elodie," he called from the boat, waving the letter above his head. "Elodie, break out the rose-mallow wine; break out the bluebottles! Lila is going to school! Everyone, everyone, Lila is going to school!"

Tubs remembered Lila's face that night, how happy she was, and how proud Aunt Elodie was. And how long the party lasted. And how they changed the words of that old song to "kiss me, I'm the smartest." And how Lila explained to them that it didn't technically make it a new song if you changed one word. And how he ate too many bluebottles. And how the turtles came over to offer their congratulations and an owl flew down and stood on the bank of the marshy expanse and talked seriously to Lila. And how the bullfrogs puffed out their necks when she walked by. But the thing he remembered the most was how she smiled. He had never seen Lila smile the way she had that night—when she was about to leave the place he loved the most.

2

That was a long time ago now and many things had changed. Tubs and Lila were grown and Elodie was gone. While Tubs lived in the same neighborhood, Lila had traveled far and learned things frogs in the swamp could only dream about.

Tubs let the cool water carry him to the boat dock, where three water rats sat quietly smoking corncob pipes and fishing. One was larger than the rest and had grizzled hair and an unruly beard. Tubs hopped out and felt the warm sun on his skin. He scratched a small itchy bump on the side of his head.

"Any luck, Virgil?" he asked the rat.

"Luck's a funny thing," said Virgil.

Tubs thought for a second, and grinned. He had just the song to cheer Virgil up! Tubs slapped his wet foot on the dock for a count of four, took a deep breath, and then burst out in a reedy voice that rang through the swamp as clear and bright as a bell.

"I know a rat who liked to sail
In sun and rain and wind and hail
He built a boat of reeds and mud
And a torn shower curtain and Persian rug
He sailed due north all through the night
A lonely firefly his only light
He docked in ports along the coast and
Served a barking seal French toast

*And all the fish and all the whales and all the wind
and all the gales*
*And all the bats and all the cats and all the crawfish
who had laughed*
Came to sing him home again
Braver than most, my ratty friend!"

Tubs clapped his hands and skipped about the dock. He hopped and clicked his heels together, then bounded forward in a high pirouette and landed in front of the rats, laughing. "Whaddaya think?"

"Tubs," said Virgil. "I ain't built no boat out of mud."

"Nah," said one of the other rats. "Boat like that would jus' fall apart."

"It's a *song*!" said Tubs. "Not instructions for building a boat."

"Hey, Tubs," said one of the rats, shifting the corncob pipe to the other side of his mouth. "Could you hand me that can of worms?"

"Rats," Tubs muttered to himself, chuckling as he left Virgil and his friends on the dock. He headed inland through the reeds to the frog hospital at the base of a giant cypress tree. Tubs stopped by the hospital most days to visit Lila and bring her some lunch. She was a doctor now, and very busy.

The waiting room was filled with frogs and toads and a crawfish and a tired-looking woodpecker who was missing some feathers.

"Mornin', Maude," Tubs said to a small red-eyed tree frog who was holding a monogrammed handkerchief to her nose. Maude must have had quite a cold because she was still wearing her pajamas and slippers, and not her usual hat or string of pearls.

"Mornin', Bernadette," he said to the crawfish, whose antennae were drooping.

"Mornin', Tubs," said Bernadette.

On his way to Lila's office, Tubs stopped in to say hello to a swallow named Gloria, who worked in the lab. Gloria had shining black eyes and a look of keen intelligence. Her feathers were glossy and dark blue. She had short legs and slender pointed wings, and always wore a tie and jacket.

Gloria was the only bird from their part of the swamp who had flown around the world. She knew many languages. Tubs liked the way she turned her head to the side quickly when she was listening, and the almost weightless way she bobbed along when she walked. No one looked more awake than Gloria.

Tubs leaned in the doorway. Gloria looked up quickly and gave him a wink. He noticed that her feathers looked a little dull and ruffled today, and her tie was loosened around her throat.

"Tubs!" she called in her beautiful voice. "Have I told you the joke about the roof? Actually, never mind, it would be way over your head." She chirped out a little laugh and then started coughing.

Tubs found Lila back in her office. She was wearing her lab coat and was hunched over a microscope. She looked up to greet him and the smile she wore was thin. Her eyes looked tired and worried.

"Tubs," she said. "I can't eat lunch with you today, I have too many patients. The whole swamp is coming down with the same cold. Especially the birds and the fish and the frogs. I spent the morning handing out cough medicine and anti-itch cream."

"Well, you gotta eat something," Tubs said. He reached into his pocket and brought out a red bandanna, which he unfolded and set on her desk. From his other pocket he took out a small jar of spicy mayflies and a little bottle of bog-birch soda, which he set on top of the bandanna.

"Thanks, Tubs," Lila said. "I don't know what I'd do without you."

Tubs pulled a harmonica from his vest pocket and

played her a song while she ate. As he played, he thought about all the broken things Lila had fixed since they were young. It was a long list—his radio, Elodie's teapot, Virgil's fishing pole, Bernadette's claw, the gate to the water rats' boathouse. . . .

Tubs's song had no words, but the way he played it, you could tell it was about Lila fixing and building things. You could just hear it in the harmonies. And though it was a new song—one he'd just made up— it felt familiar and old. When Tubs was done playing, Lila's eyes looked brighter and she didn't seem so tired. He knew she felt better because she began explaining how the microscope worked to him, but Tubs couldn't really listen because a new song was sailing into his thoughts.

"That's amazing!" he said to his cousin, walking closer to the door. "How about that?" he said, turning the knob. "I wonder who thinks of these things," he called as he skipped down the hallway and back out into the reeds.

A new song was nothing to ignore. He had to get home and capture it before it got away.

3

By the time the moon had risen, shining silver on the dark water, Tubs was still at his piano. He'd lit the lanterns on his porch and a small gathering of moths fluttered around them, listening to him play. The water lapped at his dock, and a breeze blew through the house, rustling the calico curtains.

He pounded out a melody with one hand, then spun around and grabbed his trombone, tapping his foot on the floorboards and letting the trombone's smooth low voice slide through the living room. He had just grabbed the washboard and was scraping it hard with a spoon when he heard a thud against his door. The next thud was followed by the sound of voices and laughing.

Before Tubs could go see what was happening, his front door burst open and a dozen boisterous frogs piled into his house, slapping him on the back. They scattered around the living room, taking up space on his piano bench and at his kitchen table. One of them—a tall skinny frog, wearing a tweed coat— went to the stove and put on a pot of chicory. Another rifled through his cupboards, taking out bags of dried mosquitoes, hot peppers, and catberry jam.

"Tubs, where you been?" said the tall skinny frog. "We've been down by the reeds waiting for you. Decided to bring the party over here."

As he was talking, more frogs showed up, along with Virgil, two turtles, and a duck. They brought bottles of rose-mallow wine and candy made from mealworms and willow sap.

"Hey, how come Lila don't come to our parties no more?" asked a frog wearing a fancy shirt with pearly snap buttons.

"I think, Beau, what you mean to ask is why *doesn't* Lila come to our parties *anymore*," said a yellow tree frog.

"That's just the kind of thing Lila would say if she were here," said the duck.

"And nah, that's *not* what I mean," said Beau. "What I *mean* is, why don't she like our music no more?"

"She does," said Tubs. "But she gets up very early now that she's a doctor."

"A doctor! I heard Lila wasn't really from here," said Beau.

"Of course she is."

"I heard at the sirbun they don't eat flies, they eat *cheese*," said Beau.

"That's disgusting!" said a turtle. "Why would you say that about anyone?"

"I heard Lila ate a *duck* when she was at the sirbun," said a wood thrush.

"WHAT?" asked the duck, rising up on his toes and beginning to flap his wings.

"Relax, Billy," said Tubs. "Lila didn't eat a duck."

"If she wasn't born here and she ate a duck," said Beau, "is she really a frog?"

Tubs pointed to a picture of Lila that was hanging by the piano.

"Oh, she *looks* like a frog," said Billy. "But that doesn't *prove* she's a frog."

"She's a frog," said Tubs. "But why does it matter if she's a frog or not?"

"I can prove she's *not* a frog," said Beau. "You know any frogs who went to the sirbun? Or who became doctors? You know any frog who can do carpentry?"

"Yeah," said Tubs. "Lila."

"See?" said Beau. "That proves it."

"Huh?" said Tubs.

"Beau," said Virgil. "You don't make no sense."

Beau sighed. "All I know is nobody can catch no fish and lots of people been getting sick since Lila came back from the sirbun. You seen Gloria lately?"

Some of the birds raised their voices in agreement.

"Gloria is sick?" said Tubs. "But I just saw her. She was telling jokes."

"She's not sick," said the wood thrush. "She's just losing some feathers."

Tubs felt relief wash over him. And then Beau said, "She's losing her feathers because she's sick—just like the woodpeckers. Before we had a doctor, no one here got sick," Beau went on. "You lost an arm, it grew back. You ate some bad mayflies, you just slept it off in the mud."

"I thought this was supposed to be a party," said Virgil. "I ain't here to listen to nonsense."

"Beau's right," said a crawfish with a missing claw. "Before Lila came back, there were hundreds of tadpoles every spring—now sometimes we have five or six."

"I bet she used some spell she learned at the sirbun," said Beau.

"The Sorbonne is a school," Tubs said. "They don't teach spells there."

"But she ate a *duck*!" the duck cried again.

A hush fell over the room and everyone looked at the door. Lila was standing there—still dressed in her lab coat from work and holding a box of crickets.

"You're right," said Lila.

The duck jumped up on top of the piano, his eyes turning dark with terror.

"Not about eating a duck, Billy," she said, shaking her head. "But Beau is right; since I came back from the Sorbonne, people have been getting sicker. We need to figure out why."

4

There was only one animal in the swamp who might answer such questions. Few creatures were brave enough to visit her, and some didn't believe in her advice at all. Still, Pythia's lineage was nearly as old as the frogs', and her house was a broken-down shack beneath the willows, where the branches of the trees were filled with muck and moss and nests. Her shack was nearly invisible because of the haze of insects and swamp gas that surrounded it.

Tubs was not afraid to visit Pythia. He believed

most creatures were good at heart, as long as they weren't too hungry. Still, he kept his journey a secret from Lila. She wouldn't want him to visit the old shack, and would certainly try to stop him from speaking to a witch.

Instead he told Virgil.

The old water rat nodded gruffly and started unmooring his boat.

"Ain't a good idea to swim all the way there," he told Tubs. "Be mighty hard to swim back if she takes a bite out of you."

Tubs and Virgil left before dawn. Virgil paddled slowly through the marsh, his corncob pipe giving off little puffs of sweet-smelling smoke.

The rhythm of the oars in the water was hypnotic. Tubs was enjoying himself, lying back in the stern and gazing up at the sky. Soon, he thought, their troubles would be over. Pythia would tell him what to do, then creatures would be well again, and Lila wouldn't have to work all the time. There would be fish and tadpoles, and parties, like before.

He began planning a great party in his head. There would be a five-piece band and dancing. There would be delicious food and special willow-sap sodas and sweet cakes and chicory coffee. He'd invite all the egrets, and all the sparrows. Everyone would make up new songs and play them long into the night. He even began composing a little song in his head, humming to himself. He was in a fantastic mood.

Tubs and Virgil had traveled together a good distance before Virgil said, "Oh, and Tubs, she's known to occasionally eat you instead of answering your question. I ain't so sure she's magic."

"Pythia won't eat me," Tubs said, grinning at his friend. "I've brought my harmonica!"

"You're going to give her the harmonica to eat?"

"Huh?" said Tubs. "Of course not! It's just that no one eats a frog with a harmonica."

"Tubs, but . . . I mean . . . ," Virgil began.

"Yes, I know, I know," said Tubs. "But Millie was a toad and she was playing a violin."

"Uh, and then there's . . ."

"Okay, yes," said Tubs. "But Franklin was playing the clarinet. That's why I didn't bring my clarinet."

"Uh . . . ," said Virgil.

"I hope you're NOT going to bring up Deedee," said Tubs.

Virgil puffed on his pipe and squinted off over the swamp. Then he shrugged.

They were coming into view of the cloud of insects, and Tubs had a light snack.

When they reached the misty border of Pythia's property, Tubs slipped from the boat into the water and swam through the deep green swamp. The light from the sun broke through the water and reached down to the mud beneath him, illuminating the gleaming stems of water lilies and duckweed and cinnamon fern.

He emerged at the edge of Pythia's dock. The smell of swamp gas was strong, like it was coming from inside. The wood creaked as Tubs crept up onto the first step of Pythia's shack. Her door was shut, but it wasn't much of a door. It looked suspiciously like someone had taken a bite out of it.

Tubs peered through the ragged door into the mist and gloom. Inside, he could see a large green creature with an enormous mouth. The pupils of her eyes were vertical lines and these strange eyes stared drowsily back at him. Tubs walked into the strange and steamy room, transfixed by Pythia's stare. He had never seen a witch before!

She was sitting on a three-legged stool, balanced directly over the source of the misty haze, and was wearing a flowing red dress. She wore sapphire rings on all her fingers. On her head was a wreath made of swamp rose.

She smiled slowly, showing three feet of sharp yellow

teeth, and Tubs trembled. Remember, he said to himself, she is a creature just like me.

"Have you brought me a present?" the witch asked.

Tubs cleared his throat. Swamp gas was going to his head and he was beginning to feel dizzy. "I have," he said.

"Very good," said Pythia. "Play it for me."

Tubs took out his harmonica and began to play—slowly at first, then with feeling, slapping his foot on the wooden floor.

Pythia listened, her eyes gleaming. Soon she, too, was tapping her foot, her long claws scratching like brushes on a drum, her enormous weight thumping down on the floor, making the furniture jump and rattling the pots and pans in the kitchen. The sound of the thumping, jangling song filled Tubs with delight.

He began to dance and the alligator witch swayed from side to side. She clapped her hands, and her rings clicked with a lovely snap. When Pythia's teakettle began whistling, it was more than Tubs could bear. He spun, enthralled by the mysterious music of everyday life, the brushing and snapping and whistling and stomping, and his own harmonic melody tying it all together.

Ravished by the beautiful noise, Tubs flipped up into a handstand, holding the harmonica with his feet, then tossed the harmonica high into the air. But before he could catch it, Pythia snapped it up in her mouth and ate it whole.

The music ended abruptly, and Tubs stood still. A hot haze hung in the room and he was sweating. Only the teakettle's shrill whistle continued to sound.

Pythia leaned down to look into his eyes, grinning so he could see every one of her sharp yellow teeth.

"Would you like some tea?" the witch asked in a low growl.

5

Tubs wished there was something cool to drink in the steamy shack, but he didn't want to risk Pythia thinking he was rude by refusing her tea. It had long been believed Pythia knew everything—that she talked to spirits, that the swamp gas gave her visions, that the creatures she ate were sacrificed in the name of knowledge. He considered himself lucky. The ancient witch had only eaten his harmonica.

Pythia returned from the kitchen carrying a dented silver teapot and two chipped china cups, which she set on the stool. She poured them each a steaming cup of murky green tea, then sat down on the floor beside him.

"Now, my bright young friend," she said, "you may ask your question."

Tubs looked in the cup and watched something dark and strange churning at the bottom. The tea smelled like mushrooms and dirt.

"My question," said Tubs, "is why are so many creatures getting sick? Why are there no fish? What happened to all the tadpoles?"

Pythia appeared lost in thought, her eyelids drooping. She breathed deeply through her enormous nostrils, her head nodding as though someone unseen was speaking to her.

Finally, she said. "Haven't got a clue."

"WHAT?!" Tubs shouted.

"No idea," said the witch.

"WHAT?!" Tubs shouted again, unable to think of something better to say.

"No. Ideeeeaaa," the witch said slowly.

Tubs jumped up, knocking over his teacup. "But this is serious," he said.

"I see the future, not the past," said Pythia, waving her hand in the air. "I don't know where the fish have gone or why birds are losing their feathers."

Pythia leaned in close to Tubs and stared at him with her strange heavy-lidded eyes. "But I do know this," she whispered. "It's not going to stop."

Tubs's breath caught in his throat, and he backed away from the witch.

"That can't be true," said Tubs.

"Oh, dear dear, my bright little friend," she said. "It's quite true; the spirits don't lie. There is only one thing that can stop it."

"What?" cried Tubs. "Tell me."

"You, Tubs Marshfield, must leave the swamp. *You* will travel to marvelous places that frogs only dream about and hear music like you've never heard before.

34

You will stand beside the greats and people will cheer your name. You will eat delicious food and drink delicious drinks and play new songs that frogs will sing for ages to come. Crowds will carry you upon their shoulders."

"But I don't—"

"It's the only way," said Pythia. "You will walk to the railroad tracks and hop on a train. You will ride through the countryside, and when the train enters the city you will jump off. You will find yourself in a glorious place, where there are parties that last for days and songs that last for centuries. That's where your marvelous life is. Not here."

"But—"

"You must do it," said the alligator. "Because if you stay, there will be only ruin and misery for everyone."

6

Tubs turned from Pythia and ran from the room, through the rickety door of the shack, and out along the dock. He dove straight back into the swamp. He swam until he knew he was far away, then popped up to the surface.

Virgil was still waiting for him in his boat, smoking a pipe and reading a book.

Tubs grabbed the side of the boat and hurled himself over, flopping into the bottom and lying there dazed and silent. He had a prickly feeling on his neck and cheeks.

Virgil put down his book.

"Tubs, you okay? That witch put a spell on you?"

"She ate my harmonica," whispered Tubs, then he started to cry.

Virgil switched his pipe to the other side of his mouth. "Cheer up, Tubs," he said. "Harmonicas are quite easy to come by. 'Magine we could have it replaced by the end of the day."

"And she doesn't know why anyone is sick."

"Well, it's a good thing Lila studied medicine, then," said Virgil. "Seems she might-could figure out why people are green around the gills . . . you know . . . get to the bottom of all this. I'm quite a believer in modern medicine. And that Lila is sure good at fixing things."

"And she said I have to leave here because if I stay, there will be ruin and misery!"

"Huh," said Virgil. "The word *here* is not so precise. Could be interpreted in so many ways. . . . Don't seem there's much of a time line for such a trip."

"She said I was going to have a marvelous life and stand beside the greats and frogs would sing my songs for thousands of years."

"Yeah, well, you know how it is," said Virgil, puffing on his pipe. "Frogs get a song in their heads, they just keep going with it—so a thousand years ain't nothing to write home about. How 'bout we head back now?"

"I love this swamp!" Tubs sobbed, covering his eyes with his hands.

"Tubs," said Virgil, "you ain't gotta *lissen* to no alligator witch."

Tubs remained in the bottom of the boat with his speckled belly facing the sky, and Virgil began to row home. In a short time, the splash of the oars cutting through the water and the songbirds calling from the trees lulled him. He could hear a melody in his head and soon he began to hum, then sing to himself.

> *"Oh, I went o-o-o-out to the witch's shack*
> *To find a way to get the old swamp back*
> *To find the fish*
> *To find the trees*
> *To find the rain*
> *To find the breeze*
> *But all I found was gloppy tea and swamp gas fumes*
>   *and misery*
> *It's not for me*
> *It's not for me*
> *I don't want that misery"*

Tubs was beginning to feel better. He bent his knees and tapped his feet on the bottom of the boat.

"I won't go down to the railroad tracks
I won't say goodbye to the water rats
I won't live alone in an old top hat
On a windy road with a feral cat and sing love songs
    to a horseshoe crab"

Tubs leaped to his feet and spread his arms as he sang.

"Tubs," said Virgil.

But Tubs wasn't listening. *"It's not for meeeeeee,"* he sang.

"Tubs," Virgil tried again. "There's a—"

The boat passed beneath a low branch, which hit Tubs in the back and toppled him from the boat. He landed in the water with a splash, then bobbed back up, laughing. The swamp was beautiful and green and nothing in the world seemed wrong to him now. No kind of pain could last when he was singing his songs.

7

That night the stars were brighter than ever, shining even in the gloaming dusky sky. The creatures gathered in boats and on lily pads, and on the leaves, and roots of trees. They surrounded Tubs's dock—waiting to hear the tale of his visit to the witch—and they whispered to one another about the secrets she might have told him.

Inside the house, Tubs was singing and cooking dinner. Lila was sitting at the kitchen table, her doctor's bag and briefcase standing on the floor next to her chair. She was looking through a pile of papers and lab results and talking to Gloria, who was perched on the back of her chair, reading intently over her shoulder.

Tubs noticed that the feathers at Gloria's neck were now gone, and a red rash was there, too. It was the first time he had seen her not wearing a tie. It must have hurt to put it on. Gloria seemed thinner than before, and her dark eyes shone bright. The wood thrush was wrong, he thought. She wasn't just losing her feathers. She was sick, too.

"There's got to be something we're missing," Gloria said.

"Every patient I saw today has the same symptoms," Lila said. "Woodpeckers, crawfish, water rats, even a dragonfly. It's unusual to see so many different kinds of animals with the same complaints. Crawfish don't get the same colds as birds."

"It's true," said Gloria. "And the lab results for birds were the same for fish and salamanders."

"Well, we're not that different from one another," Tubs said. "We all live in the same swamp."

Tubs put bowls of soup on the table for Lila and Gloria and gave his cousin a little nudge. He had already set the table without them noticing, using Elodie's special silverware—the kind with engravings of flies on the handles. He set out three small jam jars full of water, and fancy linen napkins.

"Time to eat," said Tubs as he sprinkled some dried mosquitoes on top of the soup. Lila smiled.

"My favorite," she said. "Thank you, Tubs, you're the best."

"Thanks, Tubs!" said Gloria, giving him a wink. "Oh, hey, Tubs," she continued. "What's worse than an alligator coming to dinner?"

"What?" he asked.

"Two alligators coming to dinner." Gloria laughed at her own joke and poured everyone a glass of willow-sap soda.

Then Tubs raised his glass. "Here's to *no* alligators coming to dinner," he said.

"You were brave to visit Pythia," Lila said.

"That's true," said Gloria. "If the word *brave* also means crazy."

The friends sat at the table amid Lila's papers and began to eat. Suddenly they put down their spoons and grabbed their jars of water, drinking quickly. Gloria gave a little shriek and flew to the sink to run water over her beak.

"Hoo-wee," said Tubs, fanning the air in front of his mouth and beginning to sweat. "Heavy on the hot peppers!"

Lila gulped down her water. She ran to the sink to get more, then stopped suddenly and stood perfectly still. "Wait!" she said, a smile breaking out on her face. "Wait! The symptoms! It's almost like everyone has eaten the same bad food."

"Hey!" said Tubs. "Bad food?"

"No, no, no. *This* food isn't bad—just hot. But the sickness—maybe it's not a cold or a virus or a disease. Maybe it's the same as you and me and Gloria feeling hot pepper on our tongues at the same time."

"Yes!" said Gloria. "And that's why a crawfish can have the same kind of sickness as a woodpecker!"

"Huh," said Tubs. "But we don't all eat the same foods."

Lila sifted through her papers, took a pencil from her briefcase, and began to write furiously. "You're exactly right, Tubs," she said. "But like you said—we all live in the same swamp!"

Gloria hopped from report to report, her shiny black eyes reading every document in a matter of seconds. "There's got to be something that all of us eat," she said.

This sounded very ominous to Tubs. The thing that

was making them sick might be the thing they needed to stay alive—food. "So if we're eating it, then we'll just keep getting sicker?"

"Right," said Lila. "And if we *stop* eating or drinking whatever it is, there's a good chance we'll get better! It's okay, Tubs, we'll figure this out."

Tubs wondered if there was a way he could help, besides making dinner and playing songs. Lila and Gloria were so hard at work all the time. He *wanted* to help. But music kept calling to him. Sometimes it was hard to think of anything else—even in the midst of the sickness. Other times he was angry that this sickness had come and distracted him from his songs. He wanted everyone to be well—of course he did. But somehow in his heart, there was nothing more important than making music.

The peepers were getting restless outside, beginning to call to one another. A thud on the door made

Tubs and Lila jump, but didn't ruffle Gloria's feathers. Then they heard Beau calling Tubs's name.

He thought of the alligator witch's prophecy. The marvelous life she described was what the swamp was like before the sickness came. There were parties and ancient songs and delicious food. He couldn't make sense of it. How could it be that he alone had to leave? How would that make things better? And what a disappointment it would be to tell everyone he had gone all the way to the witch's shack and learned nothing at all.

Tubs sighed. "I guess it's time to tell everyone what Pythia said."

"Good luck," said Gloria.

"Won't you come with me?"

Lila looked up from her papers. "Sorry, Tubs. We have to get to the bottom of this, and besides, last time I saw Beau and Billy, they were yelling that I wasn't from the swamp, that I ate a duck, and that I caused the mysterious illness. So . . . you go on without us."

Tubs went to the sink and washed his dishes, then rummaged through his instruments until he found his bow and fiddle. Then he strode through the door, out into the waiting darkness.

8

The moon was still low, close to the horizon, and the sky was pale blue like the heart of a flame. Billy the duck bobbed in the water and Beau sat in his boat. The peepers stopped their calling, and the owls and birds stopped their restive evening songs; a hush fell upon the creatures as they waited for Tubs to speak.

Tubs listened to this silence. It was so beautiful. And he thought about how the notes of songs are separated by short or long silences, and how silence is sometimes the best part of a song.

The silence didn't last, though.

"What did the witch say?" yelled Beau.

"Tell us!" cried Billy.

Tubs lit the lantern that hung from the side of his house and then sat on the dock with his feet hanging in the water. All the creatures gathered closer. As the light shone upon them, Tubs could see many of them were shivering and had blankets thrown over their shoulders, their faces looked pale, and some of them had an itchy, uncomfortable-looking rash. They gazed up at him with great hope and anticipation.

"Tell us everything she said!" called a swallow from her mossy nest. "Is there a curse on the swamp?"

"What?" said Tubs. When did they come up with that crazy idea? he thought.

"Pythia said there's a curse on the swamp?" called a bullfrog from the mud.

"There's a curse on the swamp!" Beau yelled.

"Who cursed the swamp?" said Billy. "Was it Lila?"

"My friends," Tubs began, "there is no curse on the swamp. I wish I could tell you why some of you are not feeling well. But the alligator witch doesn't know."

Tubs heard the sound of many creatures gasping at once. How could he explain that Pythia couldn't answer their questions? That she was just a hungry alligator, drinking mushroom tea in a shack beneath a willow tree? Honesty seemed the best way forward. His neck felt itchy and he reached up and scratched it with a toe. He cleared his throat.

"Pythia is just a hungry alligator drinking mushroom tea beneath a willow tree," Tubs said. There was another gasp. "But," he said, "*Lila* might have an answer."

"What did Pythia say?" Beau yelled again.

"She didn't have a reason or a cure," Tubs said. "She just said that I should leave the swamp. That everyone would be miserable if I didn't."

"Then it's *you!*" cried Billy the duck. "You're making everyone sick. She's trying to save us from you!"

"Billy," said Virgil, "that don't make no sense. Why would you think an alligator, who is our natural predator, is trying to save us?" He shook his head. "I'm afraid that's a logical fallacy."

"Maybe if we figure out what she means," said Beau, "we'll get to have what *she* has!"

"*She* has a broken-down shack in the worst part of the swamp," said Virgil.

"And we don't have any shack!" cried Billy.

"What else did she say?" called a young frog from the roots of a mangrove tree.

"She said I was going to have a marvelous life and creatures would sing my songs if I got on a train and went to the city," said Tubs. "But I already have a marvelous life. And that doesn't answer our question."

"Maybe you have to go to the city to find a cure for us," called a woodpecker from the top of a willow.

"Maybe if you leave, that will break the curse Lila put on the swamp!" called a bullfrog from the reeds.

"Why would Lila curse the swamp to make people sick when she lives *in* the swamp?" said Virgil.

There was a moment of silence as the creatures seemed to be considering this. Tubs watched a cloud drift slowly over the gleaming crescent moon.

Finally, someone shouted, "Maybe when Pythia said marvelous life, she really meant *we* would have marvelous lives after Lila's curse was broken."

"That's right!" yelled Beau.

Tubs sighed. "Friends," he said. "I don't know what Pythia meant. But there is no curse on the swamp and an alligator doesn't make decisions for what *we* do. We all make those decisions together. Lila and Gloria are trying to figure out why people are sick," said Tubs. "And they need to know what we've all been eating."

"I'll tell you what Lila's been eating!" yelled Billy.

Virgil shook his head, stuffed a clump of swamp moss into his pipe, and began rowing home.

"Tubs," said a small yellow tree frog quietly. "I think

you would have a marvelous life in the city. I think you should go. Like Elodie did. No one was sick back then. Maybe there *is* some magic at work. And if there isn't, at least you can bring our songs into the world, so they won't die here in the swamp with us."

Everyone was quiet then, and Tubs felt like he might cry.

"No one is going to die here," said Tubs. But he knew it wasn't true. Not one fish jumped to catch an insect as it skimmed the surface of the water. He knew that most of the fish had died. He knew that some of Virgil's cousins who worked on the docks had died, too.

He looked out at his friends. They were sitting or treading water or floating or perched in trees in the most beautiful place in the world. But they looked haunted now, dark circles under their eyes, toads with dry skin, sparrows losing their feathers. And Gloria sitting back in the kitchen, feverish, her raw skin covered in a rash, trying with all her might to find a cure. She must feel so horribly frightened, Tubs thought, getting sicker with no cure in sight. And for the first time, he wondered how long it would be until he became sick, too.

In his heart of hearts, all Tubs wanted was to write a song that could make everyone well. If there was any magic in this world, he thought, please, *please* let that melody come to him.

9

Gloria and Lila stayed up all night reading patient reports and trying to figure out if there was something all the animals had been eating or drinking to make them sick. In the morning, instead of playing his fiddle or clarinet, Tubs went with them from house to house asking their patients what they'd put in their bellies that month. Gloria was weaker now. The rash on her talons made hopping and walking painful, but she was determined to go with them, flying when she could muster up the energy.

The three friends talked to nearly everyone in the swamp except for Billy, who slammed the door in their faces, and Beau, who said he didn't believe Gloria was really a sparrow.

"You look like a wren," he said.

After talking to dozens of different creatures, they collected samples of water and algae and bugs, then Lila and Gloria took their papers and notes and collections of specimens and went straight to the lab at the hospital. Tubs went home to make lunch for everyone.

They had learned that most animals in the swamp ate bugs, even other bugs. Some ate them by mistake; some, like Tubs, made fancy fly soufflé. Birds and frogs—who were the first to get sick—ate the most bugs. But in the end, not everyone ate bugs.

They also learned that most animals ate plants. And very nearly everyone ate the delicious green algae that covered the swamp.

All animals drank water and ate microscopic crea-tures—creatures too small to see.

Water was the thing that connected everyone. He thought again of the fish. How he had come across some while he was swimming, bumped right into a whole school. They were floating, dead, just beneath the surface of the water, their round eyes still staring at the sky. He shivered at the memory.

What if Pythia was right? Would there be more animals dying if he stayed? Would there be only misery like she had told him? All animals had to die someday, he thought, but not all at once, and they shouldn't have to suffer.

Tubs went first to give Gloria her lunch in the lab, but she was nowhere to be found. He assumed he would find her in Lila's office.

The halls of the hospital were crowded—with sick patients lying in cots. The hospital was too full for them to stay in rooms.

Tubs let himself into Lila's office and was surprised to find her alone.

"Where's Gloria?" he asked.

"She had a fever," Lila said. "Virgil came to pick her up in his boat and take her home."

"Will she be all right?" Tubs asked.

"Of course she will," said Lila. She turned away quickly. "We're getting closer. We know that eating algae or bugs or plants is making us sick, but what are the algae, the bugs, and the plants eating that's making them poisonous to us? The things that the smallest creatures eat still get into our bodies and can make us sick. Once we know what they are . . ."

"How do we avoid eating things that make us sick if we can't even see them?" Tubs asked.

"We find the source of the problem," Lila said. "We find where the poison is coming from. Where do the creatures who are sickest live?" she said. "Creatures like Gloria." Her voice caught in her throat, and she looked away again.

Tubs put his hand on Lila's shoulder. "She's going to get better," he said.

Lila nodded, and he took her lunch out of his bag and put it on the table. Neither of them felt much like eating after that conversation.

He'd brought her fresh baked cricket bread and mealworm butter. "You still have to eat," Tubs said. "And you still have to sleep."

Lila nodded.

"Hey, Lila," said Tubs, imitating Gloria's melodic voice. "Why do hummingbirds hum?"

Lila broke into a little smile and wiped her eyes. "Why?" she said.

"Because they forgot the words."

Lila laughed and shook her head. She sniffed and then blew her nose. When she bit into the sandwich, her eyes grew wide. "This is delicious. It's just what I needed, Tubs. Thank you."

"Gloria is going to get better," he told her. "I'll do everything I can to make sure."

Lila nodded. "Me too."

"I didn't get a chance to play my fiddle last night," said Tubs, reaching into his sack and pulling out the bow and violin. "Would you like a little lunch tune?"

"Of course," she said.

Tubs put the fiddle to his ear and raised his bow, drawing it across the strings. It was a pleasure to play. The sound was rich and full of life like the voice of someone who was about to laugh. As he drew the bow across the strings, he thought about all the things that Lila knew, and he thought about how a song was like a dream, how sometimes you didn't know where it would go because it had a life of its own.

Tubs wondered if Lila's studies and observations

had a life of their own—if they moved through her like the song moved through him. Maybe songs and ideas floated free in the air—and sometimes they caught a body that could bring them into the world. Maybe Gloria's jokes caught her so she could tell them.

This is a song of dreams, Tubs thought, and as he played, he watched Lila's tired head droop. Then she leaned forward and rested her head on the desk. By the time the song was done, her golden eyes were closed, and she was adrift in sleep.

Tubs packed up his bandanna and fiddle, then headed home to plan a going-away party.

Things were going to get better, he knew it. As long as there was music in the world. He just needed to find the right song. And play it in the right place.

As Tubs walked, he hopped up and clicked his heels together, humming the refrain of his newest song.

It's not for meeee,
It's not for meeee,
I don't want this misery.

He couldn't let anything happen to Gloria. He couldn't let her suffer. If there was any chance Pythia was right, he'd have to take it.

10

The first song Tubs ever wrote was called "Baby Owl." He still had a tail then and his family still called him the tadpole. The song was a lullaby and went like this:

Up above the world so magic and free
I love you, baby owl, I hope you have a good rest
Up above the world, up above the sky
Magic surprise

He sang the song sitting on Elodie's lap and Lila sang harmony, and the old frogs laughed and played fiddle and piano. Later, while he and Lila were sitting in the red-and-white boat, his uncle, an ancient bullfrog with a large downturned mouth, came out to the dock.

"You children got a gift of voices," his uncle said. "But you gotta be careful singing songs to owls. They'll come down straight outta the night sky and carry you off, eat you up in one gulp. You be careful who you sing to," he said.

Tubs shook the memory away. He hadn't seen an owl in the swamp since Lila had left for school. He would love to see a baby owl now.

He looked in the mirror while he brushed his teeth and pulled the collar of his plaid shirt up to cover the bumpy red rash on his neck.

Out in the kitchen, Tubs had prepared a feast using all the reserves from the pantry: jars of pickled sea lettuce, fiddlehead ferns, mealworm butter on tiny round crackers, a steaming spicy stew. He'd cooked all afternoon through the heat of the day, and sent word around for everyone to arrive before sunset. For dessert he had made a cinnamon cake with green and gold icing.

Now Tubs busied himself tidying the house, mopping the floor, and dusting the windowsills, straightening the paintings on the walls. He wanted everything to be perfect for his last day in the swamp. He didn't want any more sadness. Tubs went to his room and folded his clothes—packing some of them up in his bandanna.

He washed the dishes, standing below the portrait of Elodie, and he wondered if he could write a song that would last two hundred and sixty-five million years. What kind of song would he sing? What would he want to say in a song that would be around for so long? Would it be a song to keep everyone thinking about the swamp? No, he thought—a song to make everyone *feel* the swamp, feel how it feels on a summer night or early in the morning with the mist rising—a song for a day when there might not be a swamp. A song to carry the swamp into the future. He could feel that song out there in the world, waiting for him. And this must be what the alligator witch had meant.

Tubs dried his hands and scratched his itchy skin and looked up at the portrait of Elodie. "What should I sing?" he asked her picture.

A woodpecker and her husband were the first to arrive. They made themselves comfortable in the living room, sitting in rocking chairs. They were followed by a family of water rats whose children stayed outside and took turns jumping off the dock into the water. Frogs began to show up, each bringing good things to eat and drink, which they set on the kitchen table. They went on through the house and picked up instruments and began to sing. A long-fingered bullfrog sat at the piano and started to plunk out a tune. Soon after, Virgil rowed up in his boat. His beard was scraggly, and white hairs showed in his brown coat, but his black eyes sparkled as always.

The sun was setting, and the sky was turning deep orange and gold and reflecting on the surface of the water. Dark shapes of trees and reeds rose in the distance like silhouettes. It was a fantastic display of color and light. The house wasn't full like it had been back in the old days—but it was a proper party. And the proper place for his newest song.

Once he'd eaten three pieces of cinnamon cake, Tubs jumped up on the piano and began to dance wildly and play the washboard. His friends cheered. Frogs and salamanders picked up more instruments and soon there was a band—with Tubs leading them all.

"Look at him go!"

"That Tubs sure can dance!"

Frogs and birds and water rats began dancing in the

living room and on the dock. Fireflies flickered above their heads out among the mangroves and trumpet vines.

Tubs threw the washboard into the sink and someone handed him his trombone. He played smooth loops and short squanks, and the bullfrog with the long fingers hammered on the piano keys. Tubs handed the trombone to a young toad in a straw hat and flipped up into a handstand.

"Go, Tubs, go!" his friends yelled over the music.

"It's true," said the woodpecker. "He really does belong in the city playing with the greats!"

"Just like Elodie!"

"Play that zydeco, Tubs!"

"Sing, Tubs, sing!"

Tubs hopped back onto his feet and began to sing.

"A yellow frog told me what to do
She said, are you in the swamp or is the swamp in you?

*Do you shine like the water, do you shine like the
  stars?*
*Do you reel around the willow trees for hours and
  hours?*
Can you live in the sun, can you live in the rain?
*Can you save a grizzled water rat by getting on a
  train?*

How do we know, do we know, do we know?
When it's time to go, when it's ever time to go?

A yellow frog told me what to do
She said the sky is green and the trees are blue
We live for a moment and then we're through
You are in the swamp and the swamp is in you.
I live in the sun, I live in the rain
I am an animal who wants no more pain
*I can save a grizzled water rat by shouting out his
  name*

In a thousand-year-old song from the windows of a
   train
And now I know I know I know
That it's time to go, that it's really time to go"

Tubs jumped off the piano, clicking his heels, and landed before his friends with his arms outstretched, smiling the brightest smile, crumbs of cinnamon cake still stuck to his face. His friends were laughing, and the music of the night was all around.

11

"Tubs," said Virgil. "I ain't that grizzled, and I'm a mite offended you think I need saving. And if I *did* need saving, I highly doubt shouting out my name from the window of a train would do it. I would hope you would take me to a doctor."

"It's a *song*," said Tubs, cutting another piece of cake. "Not instructions on how to save a water rat. It's a goodbye song."

"A what?" cried the woodpecker.

"A goodbye song," said Tubs. "I'm going to the city."

Now the room was quiet and there was only the sound of the insects outside.

"I thought you didn't believe in Pythia's prophecy."

"I don't believe Pythia can tell the future," said Tubs. "I know that y'all believe in her—well, not you, Virgil, but most of y'all. I respect the decisions of everyone here, and maybe she *is* right, and maybe I'll find the thing that will make us better. It's too big a risk to ignore her warning. Besides, I can bring our songs to the city. Who knows what kind of luck that will bring us?"

"Did she say *when* you had to go to the city?" asked the bullfrog with the long fingers.

"No," said Tubs. "But I know it's time."

When Lila came home from work, the party was still in full swing, but Tubs's bandanna was packed and waiting in the red-and-white boat.

As soon as he saw his cousin, Tubs grabbed a plate from the cupboard and piled it with fiddleheads and cinnamon cake and handed it to her. He poured her a glass of bog-birch soda.

"Thanks, Tubs," she said.

They went out on the dock and climbed into the boat together like they had when they were young, and Lila ate hungrily.

"It's nice to hear music so late into the night," she said.

"It's nice Billy and Beau didn't come to the party," said Tubs.

Lila smiled. She said, "I hope they're okay."

"Lila," said Tubs. "Did you find any more answers?"

"I'm afraid not," she said. "But I did find this." She reached into her pocket and pulled out a small rectangular box and handed it to Tubs. Inside was lovely gold harmonica.

"Lila!" Tubs said, jumping to stand in the boat and

sending it rocking from side to side. "Where did you get it? When did you have the time?"

"I ordered it from a store in the city," she said. "Try not to feed it to an alligator."

"This is the best going-away present, ever," said Tubs.

Lila laughed. "Oh no, Tubs. You're not taking those things Billy and Beau said seriously, are you?"

"Of course not," he said. "I'm just doing more research—like you. I need to figure out what the witch's prophecy means or if there's something to it."

"Oh, Tubs," said Lila. "There's no prophecy."

Tubs lay on his back in the boat and looked up at the stars. "Life's mysterious," he said.

"Are you going to say goodbye to Gloria?" she asked.

"Of course," said Tubs.

"I'm gonna miss you," said Lila. "But you really do belong in New Orleans, just like Elodie—not for some crazy fortune-teller, but because you can really sing.

You know, getting out of the swamp and going to Paris was one of the best things I ever did. I want you to go, too. It might be too late for the swamp, but you could be healthy."

"Will you come with me to the edge of the swamp?" Tubs asked.

"You're not going to say goodbye to everyone else?"

"I sang them a song!" he said.

Lila put her plate down and picked up the oars. They pushed off from the dock and she rowed north beneath the stars, following the path of moonlight on the water, listening to the sweet sound of Tubs's harmonica rising into the night.

Gloria had built a lovely house in the hollow branch of a mangrove that overlooked the coastline, farther from the interior of the swamp. Tubs and Lila docked among the roots and climbed together into the branches,

making their way up to the round door. They knocked twice and then let themselves in.

Gloria's house was cozy. There was a soft couch in the center of the room, and woven rugs. Paintings of meadows and barns and reedy marshes hung on the walls. It smelled like sweetgrass and seeds inside and there was a dim lamp burning. On a small table beside the couch there were bottles of pills and tubes of arnica balm and discarded tissues.

Tubs looked around at Gloria's lovely things. Gloria herself was so small and frail now, he didn't notice she was lying on the couch beneath a pile of blankets. Then Lila brought him over to sit beside her. Gloria's bright black eyes seemed dull and distant. She was very thin, and her white skin shone pale beneath her remaining feathers. The red bumpy rash had spread across her chest. She was resting fitfully, shivering and pulling the covers up around her. Tubs put his cool hand on her forehead. Gloria looked up at him.

"You're going to feel better soon, Gloria," he said. "I know you are."

"Thanks, Tubs," she chirped hoarsely.

"I'm going to the city to see if Pythia's prediction is right," he said. "Soon you'll be out flying again."

Gloria nodded and closed her eyes. "Good luck."

Then she was very still and it frightened Tubs. There were no sounds coming from the trees in that part of the swamp, no music from peepers or calling of night birds. A terrible dark silence enveloped them in the dim little room as he watched his friend shiver in her sleep.

PART TWO

Magic Melodies
for Everyday Life

12

Lila pulled the boat into a little cove at the edge of the swamp and told Tubs to write when he arrived in New Orleans. She gave him a little tube of arnica balm to put on his rash.

"This will stop the itch," she said. "Hopefully in the city, you won't get sicker."

"How did you know?"

"I'm a doctor, Tubs; putting your collar up wasn't fooling me. Plus, you've been scratching your neck with your toe for half an hour. If it keeps up, go to a doctor in New Orleans. I hear there are many good frog doctors there. If my theory is right, though, you should be feeling better once you are out of the swamp."

Tubs rubbed some of the cool balm on his skin. He was frightened of becoming as sick as Gloria. And yet he was sad to think that he would be getting out and getting better while his friends stayed behind. It was a bad feeling.

Lila said, "Once I've found the source of the problem and people are well again, I'll come and hear you play."

Tubs hopped off the boat onto dry land and watched Lila row back to their home.

When she was out of sight, he headed north inland, toward the railroad tracks.

The sun was coming up, sending golden beams through the clouds. The land was hard beneath his feet. He walked for a long way—feeling the air getting warmer. He opened his mouth to sing but something in him didn't want to. He thought about his friends in the swamp, dancing even though they were sick, and it made him smile. Then he thought about the ones who couldn't come out and dance at all.

His breath caught in his throat. Please let the right song come to me, he thought.

He headed away from the water and traversed a wide field bordered by a little wood. Copses of thick scraggly bushes and trees lined his path and he walked for some way before he realized he was thirsty. Tubs had never really felt thirst before. He'd never been this far from the swamp. He put another glob of arnica balm on his skin to keep it wet and cool.

The grass on the trail got higher and soon it didn't look like a trail at all—or at least not one that many animals used. He turned around and looked at the sky, hoping to navigate by the position of the sun, but it was directly over his head.

Finally, when he thought he couldn't walk any farther, he saw a little house. It was tucked into the underbrush and its roof was covered with kudzu. Tubs jumped into the air and clicked his heels. A winding brick path led to the door of the house, which was painted deep blue. The top floor had a beautiful wraparound balcony, and he wondered what kind of creature lived there.

Tubs knocked and waited. After a moment he heard a voice from just above.

"Yoo-hoo! Frog!"

Tubs adjusted his gaze and saw a round creature with brown fur and long whiskers, no larger than a vole, standing on the balcony and waving. The animal had bright dark eyes and a friendly smile and was wearing a purple bedsheet like a cape.

"Hello!" said Tubs. "I'm afraid I got lost looking for the train."

"Lost?" The creature hurled itself off the balcony, and Tubs could see that the corners of the bedsheet were tied to its shoulders and ankles. The sheet poofed

out as it caught the air and the animal floated slowly to the ground, gliding to land at Tubs's feet.

"That was fantastic!" said Tubs.

"*You're* fantastic!" said the creature in delight. "I've never seen a frog with a white beard before!"

Tubs reached up to touch his face. "Oh, this isn't a beard," he said. "It's arnica balm. Makes you less itchy."

"I see," said the creature. He looked disappointed. "I thought maybe it was a disguise, and you had robbed a bank and needed a place to hide until you met up with the rest of the robbers. Or maybe you were working with a traveling theater company and that's your costume. Or the circus! It would have been so wonderful if it was the circus."

What a strange creature, Tubs thought.

"I'm Tubs," he said, holding out his hand to shake the creature's paw.

"Pleased to meet you," said the small animal. "I'm Roy. Come on in and rest for a while—it's hot out there."

13

Tubs ducked his head to get through the door of Roy's house. The inside seemed much bigger than the outside. The walls were painted yellow and there was a desk in the center of the room covered in papers, drawings, pens, pencils, a ruler, and a paintbrush.

Roy took off the bedsheet and gave Tubs a glass of water.

Tubs drank one glass, and then another, and then he poured a little over his head to cool down.

The walls of Roy's living room were covered with

paintings and photographs of small bright-eyed creatures. A large roll of paper was spread out along the floor with tiny illustrations and mathematical equations on it.

"If you don't mind me asking," said Tubs, "are you an artist or a scientist?"

"No, no, no." Roy laughed. "I'm a southern bog lemming!"

"Huh," said Tubs. "But you don't live in a bog?"

"*I* don't, no," said Roy. "The others certainly do. They really like to do everything together. But I like to get *away* from the crowd."

As the lemming talked, Tubs thought about how he did *not* like to get away from the crowd. He would like to be back with his friends right now.

"Are those your drawings?" Tubs asked.

"They're not really drawings," Roy said. "They're more like ideas for inventions."

"What sort of inventions?" Tubs asked.

"Parachutes for small animals," he said. "The bedsheet doesn't always work—I'm hoping to make one that's foolproof. Where are you headed?"

"To New Orleans," said Tubs. "And I have to get there soon."

"Oh!" said the lemming, his eyes bright. "The city! Where you can stay up all night listening to jazz. And dance! And eat delicious cakes and shaved ice with custard! Wouldn't it be wonderful," Roy said, "if you went there and you ate at a bakery? And the cake was so good you just had to meet the baker to say thank you? And then when you saw each other, you fell in love? And the two of you took a steamboat down the river and docked in the harbor? And while you were there you heard about a contest to make the best pralines? And the baker entered the contest and the prize was one million dollars and your *own* airplane? And the baker won, and the two of you got to fly to Paris and live by the river?! I think it could happen."

Tubs had never heard of shaved ice with custard. Roy's sure got a lot of interesting ideas, Tubs thought.

"Have you been to New Orleans?" Tubs asked.

"I have," said Roy. "There are strings of beads hanging from the trees, and places to eat spicy delicious seafood. There's a party just before spring that lasts for days. And the streets have beautiful names, and there's music music music. And everyone is different from everyone else."

"Sounds like heaven," Tubs said.

"No," said Roy. "I think heaven is green and full of mist and water and dappled sunlight."

"That sounds like the swamp where I come from," said Tubs.

"To each his own heaven," said the bog lemming. "Maybe the city will be yours."

"Well, thank you for the water," said Tubs, "but I should be going—I have a train to catch."

"Wait!" Roy's eyes were sparkling with a new kind of

friendly delight. "Wouldn't it be lovely," he said slowly, "if *I* had magical powers? And you could rub the tip of my nose and count to eight and it would transport you anywhere in the world you dreamed of, in just one instant? And you didn't have to take the train—and once you were there, as soon as you appeared on the street, you could make one wish—any wish at all—and it would come true?"

Suddenly, it all made sense, Tubs thought. This strange creature, who had traveled so far, and who lived completely alone in a beautiful little house in the middle of nowhere, gliding down from his balcony, inventing parachutes, talking about all his dreams and visions and big ideas. Of course, he must have magical powers! Tubs could just *dream* to be in New Orleans.

"Yes!" said Tubs. "Yes! Let's do that!" And as soon as he got to the city, Tubs thought, he would use his wish to make the sickness go away. And everyone would be happy. Maybe Pythia was right.

Roy smiled and clapped his paws. "Okay!" he cried. "Let's go!" He leaned his nose toward Tubs, his whiskers quivering.

Tubs closed his eyes and rubbed the end of Roy's nose.

He counted slowly to eight and then opened his eyes.

14

Roy stared back at Tubs, the big grin still on his face. Tubs looked around.

They were standing in Roy's living room.

"It didn't work," said Tubs, a lump rising in his throat.

"No," said Roy. "It didn't. I'd never tried it before—I guess I don't have magical powers—or not that kind anyway. Maybe it only works the third time you try it? Or maybe it only works the three hundredth time you try it! I really don't know."

Roy gave Tubs a large canteen of water and walked him back to the road that led to the train tracks. The world outside the swamp was dry and hard and bright.

"Good luck in the city!" Roy called as Tubs made his way down the road.

Tubs took out his harmonica and played a tune. Roy was one of the strangest creatures Tubs had ever met—with his visions of the future, and his whiskers quivering while he spoke. It was a shame he wasn't magical, Tubs thought.

He wondered if he acted like Roy sometimes. If he was kidding himself—dreaming of a song that could make people better, or of a song that could last two hundred and sixty-five million years.

Soon Tubs could see the steel rails of the train tracks gleaming in the sun. People were lined up at the brick station house to buy tickets, holding suitcases, fanning themselves in the heat. The animals who hopped trains, and who understood how to live without money, were beginning to line up near the edge of the tracks. Tubs went and stood with them.

There was a star-nosed mole wearing a pair of dark glasses and carrying a small round suitcase. Five salamanders dressed in identical dark suits also waited for the train.

Tubs took out his harmonica and played while he waited. The sound of the music called the salamanders over and soon they were forming a circle around Tubs. They clapped in rhythm, then began to make up a song. Their voices rose—each one distinctly different, but perfect as one sound. They were like a living harmonica, Tubs thought. The timbre of their voices carried all the mystery and excitement of meeting a new friend. Their harmonies drifted through the train yard and lifted Tubs's spirit.

"Froggy by the train track with the long white beard
Tell us, tell us, is the train comin' near?

Is it rolling down to get us through the sky so clear?
Or is it time to ride to Texas on a little spotted deer?

Froggy by the train track with the bindle stick
Tell us, tell us, how'd you get so quick?
Did you learn to dance from angels on the head of a pin?
Or did you race along the river till the ice got thin?

Froggy by the train track so bright and green
Tell us, tell us what you have seen?
Have you come to the city to be its queen?
Or is this just a little trip to buy some shaving cream?

Froggy by the train track with the golden eyes
Tell us, tell us how you got so wise
Have you listened to the bullfrogs have you listened to
    the flies?
Have you held the hands of sailors as the seas began
    to rise?

Or did your smarts come from the joy of eating sweet
    potato pie?"

The salamanders finished their song and smiled at Tubs, slapping him on the back.

"You're all right, Santa Frog!"

"Oh," said Tubs. "This isn't a beard."

"Well, you're still all right," said the tallest salamander. "And you sure can play the harmonica."

"What's taking you to New Orleans?" said the shortest salamander.

"An alligator who can see the future thought it would be a good idea because everyone in my home is getting sick," said Tubs.

"Huh," said the shortest salamander. He turned to the fattest salamander. "Didn't that same thing happen to Ruby?" he asked.

The salamanders all nodded. "Sure did," said the fattest salamander. "Exact same thing, 'cept it wasn't an alligator, it was a shooting star. And nobody was getting sick; she left because the new factory made too much noise."

"Ruby sure hates noise," said the shortest salamander.

Tubs said, "What's a . . ." but the rest of his words were interrupted by a deafening whistle and steady chug of the train and then the screech of brakes. The train pulled into the station: a racing magnificent machine. And there was a great bustle of people and animals disembarking and running to get in line.

The star-nosed mole and the salamanders lined up where they wouldn't be trampled by human feet—ready to board the train. Tubs joined them.

People made quite a racket shouting goodbyes, trundling their suitcases along, handed their tickets to the conductors. Some of the train cars were made for people, and some were just open cars with no seats that carried crates and boxes. Tubs watched as the mole and the salamanders scurried along the side of the rail and then jumped up, grabbing a metal bar at the base of the wide-open train car. They swung themselves upside down and into the train. Tubs followed, taking a running leap, and managed to jump all the way from the ground into the boxcar.

"You're a natural, Santa Frog!" said the skinniest salamander.

Surrounding the boxes and crates were a number of animals heading to the city. Some, like Tubs, carried their belongings in a handkerchief tied to a stick. Others sat on large steamer trunks.

I wonder where they are going and why they are leaving their homes, Tubs thought.

Some of the animals were frogs who nodded politely at Tubs, but there were also rabbits, a family of shrews, and a friendly-looking weasel with round glasses and tousled hair who leaned against the wall, reading a book. The weasel looked up at Tubs and smiled.

"You might want to hold on to something," he said.

The train began to roll ahead, first slowly past the station, then faster and faster. Tubs felt the wind on his skin. The countryside was rushing by—and he could see fields and buildings racing past, gone in the blink of an eye. He could now see the swamp from a distance. It was shocking to see that it was bigger than he thought, and even more beautiful and green.

The mole busied himself reading a newspaper. The salamanders started up a new verse to their song about Tubs. The shrew children played a game with chalk, drawing on the floor of the boxcar, and the weasel seemed lost in a daydream. None of them were very concerned with the world outside.

But Tubs stared, transfixed by the view, and the swamp sang to him, calling him back. What am I doing? Tubs thought. This is no time to leave the swamp. Abandoning my sick friends, listening to a creature that would just as soon eat me.

There was no other place where people sang the same songs for thousands of years, or had parties that lasted for ages. There was no other place where he stood beside the greats—it was there—in his own green home. "I'm in the swamp and the swamp is in me," he whispered.

"Hey, Santa Frog," called one of the salamanders. "You're getting too close to the door."

Tubs looked back at the animals in the boxcar and smiled. "Oh, I'm all right," he said.

And then, just as if he were hopping off his own dock on a hot summer day, Tubs jumped right out the door of the boxcar. He heard the other creatures shouting his name, but it was too late. The wind caught him, and he was flung by the force of the moving train far out over a field and into the open air.

15

The ditch was wet and full of reeds and Tubs woke groggy, with a large lump on his head. The train was long gone, taking his bindle stick and his new friends with it. He had only the clothes on his back and his harmonica, which had miraculously landed beside him in the ditch.

Tubs lay still and looked up at the sky. The air was cooler than before and the clear blue was giving way to thunderheads, gray and roiling across the heavens.

Well, he thought, here's one bit of luck at least. He tucked his harmonica in his pocket as the rain began to fall, pattering on the grasses and leaves around him, soaking his dry skin and giving him strength.

Rain has a way of making decisions for frogs. The water played a silent melody that he could hear with his whole body—and it was calling to him, like the swamp. He stood and surveyed his surroundings. He couldn't see the swamp or station house or even the railroad tracks, but it didn't matter. He climbed out of the ditch. Before him, winding away into the distance, was a narrow, muddy trail.

The song of the salamanders was still ringing in his head, and he hummed it and let his senses guide him. He didn't take the trail at all but went as fast as he could through a field of grasses until the earth started getting cooler and even wetter beneath his feet. He entered a thick hedge and came out on a muddy embankment; it was the last solid land. There before him lay the swamp—in all its green and reedy glory.

There is magic in the world, Tubs thought. But it doesn't come from rubbing the nose of a lemming or taking advice from an alligator.

Before him a forest of cattails rose out of the edge of the swamp and he headed quickly to it. He could see the glinting water and clusters of wizened trees. The thought of swimming was a comfort.

He hopped south along the bank. This will take me to the spot where Lila dropped me off, he thought, and from there it's a straight shot across to home.

Thunder shook the world, and he walked for a time in the shallows. As he walked, his feet grew itchy, and even though it was raining, his eyes grew itchy, too. Just before the place where he and Lila had docked, he reached a large mound of kudzu. Tubs decided to jump over it and hopped high above the green climbing plant. But not high enough. His legs became tangled in the vines, pulling him down onto something hard that made a very loud clang.

Kudzu does not clang, said Tubs to himself. He stomped his foot into the mound of kudzu and it clanged some more. He slid off the side and cleared away the weeds so he could get a better look.

Beneath the kudzu was a metal pipe. Tubs walked along beside it, deep into the tall forest of cattails, until the land grew marshy and softer. The farther he walked, the more his eyes began to sting and itch.

Soon he heard the sound of rushing water. He followed it down the embankment, where he saw at last the end of the pipe. From its mouth rushed a dark, glittering, foul-smelling liquid. He could see a great pool of the stuff pouring into the swamp, spreading out into the water, turning it murky like the bottom of Pythia's teacup.

"Who could have put this here?" Tubs said to the

rain. Why would anyone pour something so terrible into the water? he thought. What kind of animal would do this? Don't they know someone lives here?

The sky turned darker and thunder echoed out along the land. Tubs picked up a stick and began hacking the kudzu away from the pipe. Then he turned and walked along the edge of it in the opposite direction, following to see where it began. He walked through weeds and tall grass, his legs sunk deep into the mud.

The rain was a deluge now and the water rose up to his waist. At times he had to cling to the pipe to keep from falling. He pressed on against the current, listening to the rain pattering against the metal and the leaves and the water with a beautiful syncopation, each playing a different note, and he wondered why there were no frogs singing in this part of the land.

He was lost in these thoughts, his head down, when he walked straight into a wall. Tubs looked up. The pipe disappeared directly into this wall, which was at least one hundred times his height. Tubs hopped upon the pipe. Some weeds and vines spread up along the wall, and he pushed his way into them and began climbing. The vines were slick with rain, but the rain itself had given him strength and soon he had reached the top. With a great leap, Tubs flung himself from the climbing vines, until he could grasp the top edge of the wall. Then he pulled himself up so he could stand.

16

The sight before him stole his breath—a vast sea of concrete, steel towers, and metal pipes spread out into the landscape and rose up into the sky. These pipes released clouds of thick, awful-smelling smoke. Tubs's heart beat fast in his chest and his skin itched and burned though it was wet from the cool rain.

A hissing, thumping sound came from the awful towers. Tubs remembered the salamanders talking about their friend Ruby, who moved because a factory was too loud. This must be it, he thought. This must be a factory. He stood frozen in horror. Nothing moved or grew or sang or spoke on the other side of that wall. We can't live with this, Tubs thought. Because it's trying to kill us.

Tubs turned and took one great leap back down. He landed in soft mud.

The rain was letting up and the sun was breaking through the clouds. He ran as fast as he could back along the pipe until he reached the swamp. But there's no way to swim, he thought. Being so close to that pipe was too dangerous. He looked frantically in the reeds and along the bank for anything he could use as a boat. Finding nothing, Tubs headed south at the water's edge, trying to distance himself from the dark liquid pouring into the swamp.

He ran along in the marshy mud, stumbling and righting himself. When he reached a grove of willows leaning out over the water, he had an idea. Tubs jumped up and grabbed a low-hanging branch. Then

he ran away from the swamp, pulling the branch tight. When it was almost too hard to keep holding, he turned and leaped into the air. The branch swung out over the water, catapulting Tubs far past the mouth of the pipe.

He landed in the swamp with a splash and began to swim as fast as he could.

By dusk he had reached a garden of lily pads not far from the roots of the mangroves. He pulled himself up onto one and lay there to catch his breath. The lilies were blossoming their white flowers and the smell of his home surrounded him. Now that he was deep in the swamp, he could hear birds warbling to one another, settling down for the evening, and then, faintly, the song of the frogs coming from every distant bank. They were singing that two-hundred-sixty-five-million-year-old song. A song Tubs knew in his bones. From his place on the lily pad, he joined in.

"*Kiss me, I'm the fattest,*" he sang quietly. "*I sing so you will know. Our tadpoles are the fattest, too, our swamp will grow and grow.*"

And then he stopped.

It's not true anymore, Tubs thought. We're still singing it, but it's not true. There are no tadpoles and the swamp is vanishing. Every night we sing this lie. All of us.

His skin itched and his eyes burned and the lump on his head throbbed. He stared up into the darkening sky, with no song in his heart.

And then he heard a sound that was music to his tired ears. The steady splash of oars breaking through the water.

Tubs sat up and saw Virgil. His hair looked patchy, but he was stout and strong as always. His pipe stuck in the corner of his mouth as he guided his boat into the garden of lily pads.

"Tubs," he said. "You're covered with lumps."

"I jumped from the train," said Tubs, and he began to cry.

Virgil took Tubs's hand and helped him into the boat, then quickly headed south, taking his friend to the frog hospital at the base of the giant cypress tree.

Lila saw the boat approaching from the window of her office and ran to meet it as it docked in the tree roots.

"What happened?" she shouted.

Tubs jumped from the boat. "I found it!" he said. "I know what the algae and the reeds have been eating. I know why the fish are disappearing. I know why there are no more tadpoles. I know what's in the water, Lila, I know!"

17

The next day, after Tubs had been bandaged and Lila had administered more arnica, the entire swamp gathered at Tubs's house.

Tubs looked for Gloria amid the crowd. He listened for her melodic warbling voice. There were turtles, frogs, crawfish, birds, bugs, and water rats, even Beau and Billy came, but their friend was nowhere to be seen.

"It's all right," Lila said, watching his troubled face. "Gloria is still with us, just too sick to leave her tree."

The creatures crowded into the living room and sat beneath the open roof, a clear blue sky shining overhead. Tubs told them about the factory and the pipe, and the dark murk that was pouring into the swamp and spreading.

"Friends," he said, "we need ideas. There won't be a song or a prophecy that can cure us." Suddenly he was thinking of Roy and all his ideas, and wishing he could invent something that would help.

"We need to find a new place to live," said an egret.

"Now hang on a minute," said Beau, "how do we even *know* the stuff coming from the pipe is bad? Maybe it's something that will help make everyone better."

"Beau," Virgil began to say, then he just shook his head and shifted his pipe to the other corner of his mouth.

"How do we know Tubs and Lila aren't making all this up?" said Billy. "They're the only ones who left the swamp and now they've got this crazy story. They're trying to scare us and make us leave, too."

"How do you *know*?" said Lila. "You don't need to believe us—just look around. Every single one of us knows someone who is sick. Or who is in the hospital."

Many of the creatures cast their eyes down, not wanting to look at all, but it was clear, especially in the light of day.

"Billy, you're missing half your feathers," said Lila. "I had to bandage the sores on your legs this morning. Almost all of us have a rash—" She held out her arm, which was covered with bright red bumps. Tubs, who had been swimming a long way through the swamp, looked more like a spotted toad than green frog. Other creatures had coughs and patchy fur and red, tired-looking eyes. "Beau, you are covered in arnica balm. Do you really think we can keep living here this way?"

"Where would we go?" asked a turtle. "If this thing is so big, how do we escape it?"

"We can start heading farther south," said the egret. "Take one of the streams."

"But what about the algae?" asked a dragonfly. "And the lily fields? And the cattails and the mangroves? And the willows? We're just going to leave them here to suffer?"

A hush fell upon the animals.

"I don't want to leave my home," said Billy.

"None of us want to leave," said a turtle. "But we've got to be practical. If the water is poisoned, what choice do we have?"

"We've been around for two hundred and sixty-five million years," said the yellow tree frog. "I think that factory should leave."

At this a cheer rose up, animals clapping and yelling.

"Yes!" said Lila. "We all want the factory to leave, but how?"

Tubs knew the poison factory beyond the wall was impossible to move. Worst of all, it had made it so the things they loved—like swimming and eating—were now killing them. The yellow tree frog was right: If *they* escaped, it would just keep hurting someone else. Tubs wasn't sad anymore. He was angry.

"There's no choice," he shouted. "We're animals, we're living things. This machine hasn't just made us sick, it's made us sick at heart. And we've got to make it stop—even if we put our bodies upon the gears and the levers or in front of the pipe. If we don't do something now, we won't be around to do something later."

Another cheer rose up.

Then Virgil said, "Tubs, I ain't putting my body on no gears or in front of no pipe—and I don't want you to neither. I think we best find a way to do it without no one getting hurt. Consider how the machine works or the laws of physics and suchlike."

Suddenly there was a commotion from the birds roosting above.

"Watch out," they cried.

"What *is* that?"

Everyone looked up and saw something black hurtling down from the sky, headed right for the open roof. As it got closer, they could see it was covered with fur.

Then a purple cloud appeared to bloom out of its back and it began to float slowly down.

It landed with a delicate thunk on top of the piano. And then it looked out at the creatures of the swamp with dark shining eyes.

18

"Roy!" Tubs laughed in surprise. "How . . . How did you . . . ?"

"Turns out," said Roy, "it works the three hundredth and sixth time you wish to be somewhere else. I've been wishing to see you since you left my house."

"This is fantastic!" said Tubs.

"*You're* all fantastic!" said Roy. "I've never seen so many frogs in one little house before! Are you all waiting for a visit from a prince who is going to take you to a castle and feed you beignets? That would be so wonderful. And then he would say, come with me and live in a lagoon, the water is so clear you can see down one thousand feet. And you would all go there and sing to a mermaid who lived in an underwater cave."

"You know this vole?" Lila asked Tubs.

"This is Roy!" Tubs said. "He's not a vole."

"I'm a southern bog lemming!" said Roy.

"And you really are magic!" said Tubs. "This is amazing! We could use some magic right now. How did you do it?"

"Well," said Roy. "I was standing on my balcony, saying I wish I was with Tubs and rubbing my nose and counting to eight, and then doing it again."

The creatures of the swamp leaned in close to listen and Roy went on. "I think I fell asleep at one point— but when I woke up, I kept doing it—only *this* time I thought very hard about where you might be and I rubbed my nose and waved my bedsheet in the air and hopped up and down. And then suddenly, out of the clear sky, there came a terrible screeching noise and then a giant bird snatched me up in its talons and flew high over the swamp! I poked it in the belly with my pencil, and it dropped me and here I am!"

The frogs and the turtles and the crawfish all looked at one another.

"Tubs," said Virgil, shaking his head. "This lemming ain't magic."

"Of course I'm magic," said Roy. "What are the chances I'd fall directly into the house of the frog I was wishing to see?"

"He has a point," said Beau.

"A point on his pencil, maybe," said Virgil.

"He does not have a point," said Lila. "But maybe he can help us."

She looked at Roy. "As you were flying from your home to the swamp, did you see machines or pipes pumping smoke into the air?"

"I did!" said Roy. "Because we flew over the factory.

It smelled terrible. I thought it might be run by giant crows—you know how crows love things that smell bad? I thought they might be manufacturing ships so they could—"

"Mmm," said Lila, interrupting him. "Did you happen to see if there were people in the factory?"

"I imagine there are all kinds of people in the factory," said Roy. "Wearing hard hats and bringing lunch pails to work and understanding the mysteries of the giant crows that hired them."

"Now listen," said Beau, "it might not be a factory at all." He sneezed and adjusted the ice pack on his head. "Maybe it's a painting of a factory that you thought was real."

"Maybe Lila runs the factory," said Billy.

Then everyone was talking at once.

"Maybe it will get hit by lightning."

"Maybe we can build a dam in front of the pipe."

"Maybe Pythia can put a spell on it."

"Maybe it will get hit by a train."

"Maybe we're all having a bad dream and we'll wake up."

"Maybe we can reverse the pipe and the goo will pour all over the factory."

"Maybe there will be a forest fire—but for factories."

"Maybe people will see us—and then they'll shut it off."

"Maybe the crows can help us."

"No one lives forever."

"Maybe it's just time to go."

19

The animals talked until it was nearly evening—and no one could agree on a plan to turn off the pipe. When everyone had gone, Lila and Tubs sat at the kitchen table. The portrait of Elodie gazed out over them with a loving smile.

Outside, they could hear the first notes of "Kiss Me, I'm the Fattest" rising into the evening air. Neither Tubs nor Lila felt like singing along. Roy sat in the living room with his pencil tucked behind his ear, trying to teach himself to play the jaw harp. A bottle of willow-sap soda sat on the table and Tubs poured three cups—one extra in case Roy decided to join them.

The swamp was misty and hazy in the afternoon. It was so peaceful, Tubs understood why some believed there was nothing wrong with the water.

"First we have to figure out a time when no people are at the factory," said Lila. "We have to find a way to shut off that pipe."

"Wouldn't it be wonderful," Roy called from the living room, "if we could write a song that would levitate the factory and put it on the moon?"

"How long is he going to come up with these ideas?" said Lila.

"I don't think he ever stops," said Tubs. "But the song idea isn't all bad."

"Oh, Tubs . . . ," said Lila.

"Not to levitate the factory," he said. "But we need to start singing something different. Listen to them out there: still singing about tadpoles, and the greenest trees, and the coolest mud, and how far we can puff out our throats. But nothing is the same anymore. I think that's why folks like Billy and Beau are so confused."

"A new song isn't going to make that pipe go away," Lila said.

Tubs sipped his soda and caught a fresh fly that was buzzing by.

"But it can't hurt," she said. "It's better than trying to get everyone to agree on what to do."

"Maybe it doesn't matter if everyone agrees," said Tubs. "As long as they are trying to shut off the pipe." Tubs thought of how everyone played different instruments in a band, and everyone had a different voice. He thought of the salamanders singing in harmony, how it made a bigger sound. "Maybe it's better for everyone to think differently."

"Maybe," said Lila. "But we need to work together."

"I know a bunch of bog lemmings who like to do

whatever anyone in front of them is doing," said Roy.

"Where are they?" asked Lila.

"In a bog," he said. "Sometimes in the woods."

"Hmm," said Lila.

"Maybe we can scare the factory away," Roy said. "That duck is sure scared of you, Lila. Maybe you can scare the factory."

"The factory is a building," said Lila. "We need to scare the people who put it there."

"Billy's scared because he thinks she ate a duck," said Tubs.

"Well, the factory won't be scared of that," said Roy, "but there's got to be something."

"What scares people?" Tubs asked.

"Lions," said Roy. "Fires, hurricanes, bears, tornadoes, alligators, loud noises, diseases, other humans, earthquakes, lightning strikes, sharks, snakes, ghosts, and magic spells. The only one we have is magic spells."

"We don't have magic spells," said Lila.

"We do have an alligator," said Tubs. "And loud noises."

"And magic *spells*," said Roy.

Lila thought for a moment. "We have this illness," she said. "That should scare them—maybe if they thought they could get sick, too, they would help us."

"We could ask them to leave," Roy said. "We'd say, Could you please leave? We are covered in bumps. You're pouring glop on our houses and our ducks are nervous. And then maybe they would say yes, we're turning off the pipe, and they would take us on vacation to the top of a mountain and we would get to look out over the whole world."

Tubs could feel an idea forming like a song, waiting to come to him. "Kiss Me, I'm the Fattest" had got him thinking. Frogs were creatures of habit, who did the same things every day. And he thought fixing something didn't happen all at once, you had to work on it every day. Even to live in your house, you had to do the same things every day, like wash the dishes, sweep the dock. Virgil went fishing every day, and Lila saw patients every day. Most songs didn't come out perfect all at once, you had to play them every day before they were right.

"What do people do every day?" Tubs said.

"Eat," said Roy. "Brush your teeth, jump off a cliff."

"You can't jump off a cliff every day," said Tubs.

Roy grinned. "You can if you have a parachute," he said.

20

Lila, Tubs, and Roy weren't the only creatures who kept talking after the meeting was adjourned. All over, the swamp animals and insects began to meet.

The crawfish gathered in their pebbled homes in the shallows; the birds roosted together at the top of an ancient cypress tree; a group of water rats moored their boats together by the lily forest and sat in conversation. The dragonflies and fireflies gathered by a lamp on Billy's porch. What they talked about, on that lonely evening, one could only guess.

Lila headed back to the hospital, and Tubs had retired to his piano, where he sat plunking on the keys—and occasionally standing on his head to help him think.

Roy, too excited to sit still, packed his purple bedsheet and headed west to the little wood at the edge of a dark bog.

Outside in the swamp, Tubs could still hear "Kiss Me, I'm the Fattest," and he played the piano to the same tune.

"Please let the right song come to me," Tubs said to the piano.

Then he called out, "I am here, idea. If you need a voice, I'm yours."

He thought of Elodie, and he thought of morning light breaking through the branches of the mangroves. He thought of swimming through the green water and seeing fish, watching the plants wave and dance as he drifted past.

Soon he began to sing. He didn't change the tune at all, he kept it.

Tubs ran out to the dock and sang the new words as loud as he could. This is our story now, he thought. This is our new love song.

"If someone doesn't hear you—even when you sing
You've got to let them know—you're a creature, not a
*   thing*
If someone doesn't see you—even when you're there
That someone won't protect you
That someone doesn't care

If a stinging stinky poison pours around your house
Through a pipe or through a smokestack, you've got to
*   shout and shout*
'Cause it's gonna make you sick—if you're a bobcat or
*   a gnat*
Or a person or a swallow or a crawfish or a rat or a

hundred-legged centipede
Talking to a cat
That pipe doesn't care if you're a person or a grouse
It isn't there to help us, it's there to push us out

So kiss me, I'm the fastest,
I can swim out to the pipe, I can stand before the
 factory in the misty daylight
We can smash that thing to pieces, we can make it go
 away
Kiss me, I'm the fastest frog to wreck that pipe today

A creature is a creature is a creature
In the dirt and the water and the air
A creature is a creature is a creature
We're alive, we're everywhere

So kiss me, I'm the fastest, I can leap into the air
We can stop the pipe from spouting

We can make it go away
Kiss me by the broken pipe tomorrow and today"

When he finished, he sang the song again. This time he heard others singing with him. He sang it a third time for good measure. The fourth time he sang it, even more voices joined. The fifth time Tubs stood in the darkness and just listened. From every bank and stone, from every dock and boat, from every place in the mud, frogs were singing the new song with the old melody.

21

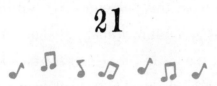

The frogs sang late into the night, and Tubs lay in bed listening.

Just as he was beginning to drift off into dreams, he remembered the salamanders, and the smart, friendly-looking weasel, and the countryside flying by. One day, Tubs thought, I'll get to New Orleans just like Elodie. One day when everyone is well again.

In the morning, Tubs got in the red-and-white boat and pushed off from the dock. He headed past the copse of young willows that had formed a canopy over a nearby embankment. Mist rose in the early light and the boat drifted along quietly. Soon Tubs could see the round door to Virgil's house, and the garden of climbing swamp moss that surrounded it. Virgil's rowboat was moored by a tall rock that jutted out of the water.

Through the mist, Tubs could see the old water rat busy at work on the muddy embankment with a group of his friends. As he got closer, he saw they weren't getting ready to fish. They were carrying great lengths of nautical rope, which they were loading onto Virgil's boat.

"Good morning!" called Tubs.

The water rats looked up and nodded.

"Mornin', Tubs! We was just talkin' about you. Frogs over this way got a new song in their heads," said Virgil.

"Yup," said Virgil's friend. "I heard frogs at the far side of the swamp started singing that new song, too."

"You wouldn't know nothing about that, now would you, Tubs?" Virgil winked.

"I didn't think you listened to our songs," Tubs said.

"Kinda hard to avoid," said Virgil's friend.

"This might-could be the first one you ever wrote that made a lick of sense," said Virgil.

"Where you headed, Tubs?" asked the first water rat.

"I'm bringing Lila her breakfast," he said, holding up a bundled handkerchief. But the truth was, he had planned to drop off Lila's breakfast and go back to the factory. "Where are you headed?"

"Aw, we're off to that pipe," said Virgil. "You know, kiss me, I'm the fastest and all that. But I don't think you'll find Lila at the hospital. She passed by here some time ago, carrying her briefcase."

Tubs rowed along the shore, thinking maybe he would see Lila and take her where she was headed in the boat, or at least give her breakfast.

The air was getting warmer and the misty fog was lifting. The red-and-white boat drifted through some high cattails where dragonflies were gathering. More dragonflies than Tubs had ever seen in his life. They must have come from far away.

"A creature is a creature is a creature!" they buzzed to Tubs as he rowed by.

"We're alive," said Tubs. "We're everywhere!"

22

Tubs kept an eye out for Lila as he rowed, but she was nowhere to be seen. Near the pebbled shore he saw a group of crawfish pushing a large stone—nearly fifty times their size. They had wedged narrow branches beneath it and were rolling it along. A blue heron and a long-legged egret walked beside them in the water, giving the stone a tremendous kick whenever it got stuck.

"Good morning," called Tubs.

Several of the crawfish waved to him; the rest kept their heads down, working hard.

The egret looked up at him and smiled with her eyes. "A creature is a creature," she said by way of greeting.

"In the dirt and the water and the air!" said Tubs, rowing on. The last time he had seen a crawfish and an egret together, one was eating the other.

The creatures of the swamp looked happier this morning, thought Tubs. The time for talking about what to do was over. Now everyone was just doing it—though he wasn't quite sure what they were doing. I wonder if Lila is at the factory, Tubs thought, because she really is the fastest.

The boat coasted along near the shallow water, and soon he was passing a little wood of ash and oak trees whose trunks grew tall and straight. Their branches reached up to the heavens and sunlight filtered through the green canopy, making patterns on the water.

On the ground between the trees stood dozens of small bog lemmings. They looked nearly identical, except for the different-colored bedsheets they wore as capes. In front of them stood Roy, holding a hammer and hopping from foot to foot. The lemmings hopped from foot to foot, too, waving their hands in the air.

"Hello!" called Tubs.

The lemmings all turned at once to see him, and they smiled.

"Tubs!" shouted Roy. "These are my friends! This is Tubs," he said to the lemmings.

There was a small chorus of "Hi, Tubs!" and "Oh, wow, that's Tubs!" and "He's so green!"

"We spent the whole night making parachutes," Roy said. "And now we're practicing our magic dance. After meeting *your* friends, I thought, wouldn't it be wonderful if some of the birds could give us a lift over to the factory? Then we could jump from their backs and glide right down and see if the people needed any help turning off the pipe. Or at least we could find where they turn it on and off."

The lemmings all nodded at once.

"And then we would turn it off and I would cast a magic spell with this hammer that would make it very hard to turn back on again."

Tubs laughed. I'll have to write a song about Roy, too, he thought.

"We already did a magic spell to call the birds," said Roy. "We stomped our feet and rubbed the tops of our heads and flapped our arms and tied bedsheets around our necks, *then* we saw Billy paddling near the bog! Our spell made him appear!"

The lemmings laughed in delight. "He just appeared out of nowhere!" "No explaining it." "There he was."

"Did you do a spell to make me appear?" Tubs asked.

"No, no, no," said Roy. "Seeing you is just a nice surprise, like seeing a cloud of butterflies when you're on your way to your sister's house to eat cake with blue buttercream icing, or finding a rock shaped like a chicken's head. But listen. Once we made Billy appear, we danced a hypnotic dance! And asked him if he and his friends would like to give us a lift. It was magic!"

"I'm not sure that's how it works, Roy," said Tubs.

The lemmings looked at Tubs. "Roy's magic!" they shouted.

"I really am magic, Tubs."

23

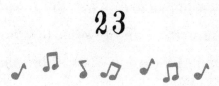

Tubs said goodbye to the bog lemmings. He steered the boat farther out into clear water to avoid a large bloom of algae, then unwrapped the bandanna and ate some of Lila's breakfast.

Fortified by the snack, he began rowing faster, taking the most direct route north. As the sun rose high, he could hear the sounds of busy creatures, and little snippets of "Kiss Me, I'm the Fastest" still being sung. The swamp echoed with animals greeting one another with the words "a creature is a creature."

Pythia was right about one thing, Tubs thought. Everyone was singing his song.

Before him a small forest of dead trees rose out of the swamp, and just as he was deciding whether to row around it or through it, he heard a familiar voice.

"Tubs, where you been?" Beau called.

Tubs looked around and saw no one.

"Up here, frog!" shouted Beau. Tubs looked to the treetops but there was no one.

Suddenly out of the hazy sky Tubs saw Billy, feet forward and wings back, patches of his feathers missing, about to make a water landing. And holding tight to Billy's back, wearing his special cowboy boots, his eyes open wide, was Beau the frog.

Billy paddled up to the boat and Beau jumped in and stood in front of Tubs, waving his arms and talking fast. The boat rocked from side to side and Tubs steadied it with his oars to keep them from tipping over.

"Tubs, you were right," shouted Beau. "That ain't no painting of a factory!"

"It's an honest to dog factory!" shouted Billy.

"And that stuff spilling out all over our home, that stuff ain't good for no one," said Beau. "We seen it for ourselves!"

"We seen a little newt all covered in that goo. He was coughing and spitting!" said Billy.

"We took him out and washed him up and helped him get on his way. But Tubs, Tubs!" said Beau. "We gotta get rid of that thing. I mean, a creature is a creature is a creature, am I right?"

"You're right," said Tubs.

"Anyways, we gotta get goin', 'cause Billy made a promise he's gotta keep." And with that, Beau hopped onto Billy's back and the two flew off over the water.

24

Tubs was right about Lila; she was the fastest.
She was there at the factory when it opened, wearing
her lab coat and carrying a briefcase full of files. She
didn't climb the wall like Tubs had but entered through
the front gate. She hopped unseen through the maze
of smokestacks and human machines until she found a
building where people came and went. Some of them
wore hard yellow hats and big boots, and some of them
wore fancy gray dress coats and ties, like her professors

at the Sorbonne, only human. Lila followed the people who looked like professors.

Inside the building it was cool and bright. The floor was smooth and the ceiling seemed as far away as the sky and she hopped until she found a room with an open door. A tall man was sitting behind a desk, writing in a large ledger. The office had a big window that looked out over the swamp and another window that looked out over the smokestacks.

Lila cleared her throat to get the man's attention, but he didn't hear her. She walked closer and hopped up on one of the chairs and said, "Excuse me, I'm wondering if we could talk."

The man didn't look up.

Finally, Lila hopped from the chair onto the man's desk. "Excuse me," she said. The man leaped up and nearly fell over. "Sorry to startle you," said Lila.

Before the man could say anything, she opened her

briefcase and began taking out folders and papers and laying them across his desk.

The man pinched himself—then rubbed his eyes. "I must be dreaming," he said.

"You look wide awake to me," said Lila.

"I'm sorry," said the man. "But unless you have an appointment, you're going to have to leave."

"I don't have an appointment," said Lila, "and I'm not leaving. My name is Lila Marshfield and I'm a medical doctor."

The man looked around. "Is this a practical joke?" he said.

"I beg your pardon," said Lila indignantly.

The man sat back down; his face was pale. "All right, Ms. Marshfield, what can I do for you?"

Lila handed him a folder. "For many springs the creatures of the swamp have been getting sicker," she said. "We have rashes and colds, and bellyaches and pain, and some of us can't stop sneezing."

"That's a shame," said the man. "Would you like to come home with me and live in my daughter's room? We have a very nice house with a frog pond in the yard. All the crickets you could eat. The frogs there are happy."

"No, thank you," said Lila. "What I'd like to do is give you a checkup."

"What?" said the man. "No, no, no. I have a doctor of my own species."

"If frogs are getting sick," said Lila, holding up her arm to show him the rash, "that means you could be getting sick, too. It means everyone could get sick."

The man laughed—and his booming voice shook Lila.

"You're pouring something into our home that's hurting us," said Lila. "But you live near the swamp, too."

"I won't be sick," said the man. "I don't swim in the swamp, I don't drink the water, I don't spend time on the shore. I just look at the pretty view—and you can't get sick from that."

"You breathe the air," said Lila. "And you've made the air foul."

"Listen, little frog," said the man.

"Don't interrupt me," said Lila. "I'm a scientist and a physician. I can tell you that if you kill the insects and the frogs and the fish and the little things no one sees—you'll be next. I'm here to ask you to shut off that pipe. It's for your own good, not just mine."

The man laughed again. "Come on back and live with my children, you can bring your whole family. I'm as sad as you that the swamp isn't safe anymore. But it's not me. I would never hurt an animal."

"You're hurting hundreds of animals," Lila said. "The swamp isn't safe because you're poisoning it."

"I can't shut off that pipe," said the man. "I'd lose my job, I'd lose my house, I wouldn't be able to feed my children. You can understand that."

Lila looked at the man. He had large blue eyes. How can he look into my eyes, she thought, and not know that we all need the same things?

"I do understand," said Lila. "There were no tadpoles in the swamp this spring."

"I can't shut off the pipe," he said again.

"Then we'll shut it off for you," she said.

25

Lila packed up her briefcase and turned to go. Out the window she could see a dark cloud gathering, but the air around her didn't feel like a storm was coming on. The cloud moved quickly. It wasn't drifting across the sky, blown by the wind; it was rising and falling as though it were flying. Lila held her breath. Could it be a tornado? she thought.

"What is that?" the man asked.

Lila said nothing. She could see the cloud was made of hundreds of birds of all sizes. Woodpeckers and curlews and gulls and terns and doves, shrikes and martins and larks and swallows, all speeding toward the factory. Each carrying something black and furry on their back. And then Lila could see Billy, half his feathers gone, the red rash covering his neck, flying fast toward the window. Just as he was about to hit it, Roy sprang from Billy's back, his purple bedsheet puffed out behind him. He raised his hand and Lila saw light glint off the hammer.

She only had time to whisper "What in the world?" before the window shattered and Roy burst into the room, skittering across the man's desk. Through the broken window came a swarm of dragonflies.

The man shouted in surprise as glass rained down around them and insects filled the air.

Roy held out his hands and waved them up at the man's face as though lightning could come from his fingertips. Billy landed beside Lila and rose up on his toes, flapping his wings at the man.

"Bobo!" Roy cried.

The man looked confused.

"Bobo!" Roy yelled again.

"What is he doing?" Lila asked.

"Scaring the factory," said Billy.

"I think the word he's looking for is *boo*," Lila whispered to Billy.

"Some people are scared by bobo and some people are scared by boo," he said. "You ain't the arbiter of other people's fears, Lila."

Suddenly, an alarm began to sound. The animals jumped in shock and covered their ears. The man looked out the window again, and then he began to run.

"Ha!" shouted Roy, dancing on the desk. "Magic! We scared him away!"

"We did!" shouted Lila. She laughed. "Now, c'mon, we can find the switch!"

Roy ran down the hall with his hammer and Lila and Billy ran after him.

All through the factory, bog lemmings were laughing in glee, climbing in windows, shutting lights on and off, opening and closing desk drawers, turning handles, flushing toilets, while people in suits and people in yellow hard hats chased after them.

26

Down in the swamp, no one would be able to tell what was going on, because from a distance the factory looked as it always did. The only strange thing Tubs noticed was that the sky was unusually full of birds. His day of drifting in the swamp had brought him to many different creatures, but other than Beau, he had seen no frogs. He'd only heard their voices, the distant melody rising into the air.

Tubs began to worry. Did they go to the pipe early, before anyone else, and get covered in goo like that newt Beau had seen? Did they get washed out into the swamp and drown or get captured by the men who ran the factory? Did his song make them do something dangerous? His heart pounded in his chest and he began rowing faster, looking out for frogs in the water and on the land.

Closer to the factory, he could smell the smoke from the stacks. The air was charged as though a storm was approaching. Tubs was tired of rowing and longed to get into the cool water and swim.

In the distance he could see a ripple of current on the water's surface, and wondered what was going on beneath it, if a school of fish might be approaching. He smiled to himself. It had been a long time since he'd encountered a school of fish.

The boat moved steadily toward the rippling water. Tubs was looking down as he rowed when he felt the boat stop suddenly. He hadn't hit a submerged rock— or gone aground—the boat simply stopped. He tried rowing harder to no avail. He turned to the stern to see if he might be caught in some weeds—and then he saw it, a green clawed hand holding tight to the leeward edge of the boat. On each finger there was a sapphire ring.

Another hand appeared and then the boat began to tip until one side was nearly pulled under. And then a large narrow head rose above the surface of the water. Its strange eyes peered deeply into Tubs's eyes, and its mouth grinned with three rows of razor-sharp teeth.

"Pythia," Tubs said, stepping back from the witch's mouth and trying to catch his balance.

"There are so many tasty creatures out and about today," said the alligator witch.

The bottom of the boat was slippery, and Tubs lost his footing. He began to slide toward the alligator's mouth, scrambling frantically. Finally, he grabbed an oar and used it to brace himself.

"And everyone headed to the same place," the witch said. "What a wonderful buffet, very convenient."

"Oh, you wouldn't want to eat anyone there," said Tubs, trying to keep his voice from trembling. "They're all—"

The witch grinned. "I told you to leave the swamp, didn't I? I told you if you stayed, all would be misery. There's still time for you to go."

"This is my home," said Tubs.

"Is it?" said the witch. "Or is music your home? Home for you is anywhere you play your songs."

How could someone so horrible say so many things that made sense? Tubs thought.

"This is where my songs began," he said. "This is where I'm singing now, so this is my home. Maybe you live too far away to hear our songs but things are different now."

Pythia let go of the side of the boat and it rocked

back into place. Her eyes glazed over and she appeared to go into a trance.

"Everyone heard your song last night," said Pythia. "My cousin in Brazil heard your song. Soon there will be no creature living by water who doesn't know your song."

"Then help us," said Tubs. "This is your home, too."

27

Pythia didn't answer Tubs. She sank back into the dark water and disappeared with a lash of her tail that sent his boat spinning and cresting on a wave. Water spilled into the boat and Tubs held on for dear life, clutching his oars to make sure he didn't lose them.

When the boat stopped rocking, he found himself by the willows that he'd used as a catapult—just a short hop downstream from the pipe. His head was still spinning, and the air was full of sound. Everywhere he looked—on the shore and in the water, in the branches of trees—there were frogs. So many more frogs than lived in his small part of the swamp. Tubs docked his boat and jumped to shore, looking through the crowd of faces for Lila. Some frogs stood still, waiting and singing, and others were headed toward the factory.

"Friends," cried Tubs. "There is a hungry alligator coming this way. You must protect yourselves, get to safety."

But so many frogs were singing his new song, they couldn't hear his warning. He shouted Lila's name, hoping she might be nearby.

Lila was not nearby at all.

Inside the factory the bog lemmings ran loose, chanting their magic spells, climbing walls and towers and stacks. The lemmings created such a distraction, Lila and Billy were able to look for a master switch. They raced past offices through the factory and down a metal staircase. Finally they reached a cavernous, steamy, foul-smelling room on the ground floor. It made their eyes sting and their skin itch. There was not a person in sight, but there were dozens of switches in the room—one of them, an enormous red dial, was encased in a glass box.

"This has got to be it!" said Lila, coughing.

The room was full of metal pipes that twisted every which way, but only one that was headed straight out through the factory wall.

"Let's wreck this thing," said Billy.

But neither Lila nor Billy nor anyone inside the factory could have known what was going on outside in the mud.

Tubs ran as fast as he could along the shore, warning anyone who would listen that Pythia was on her way. "There's no knowing what she'll do!" he shouted.

At a forest of cattails, Tubs ran into the yellow tree frog, carrying a backpack full of stones.

"Pythia might be coming," he told her.

The tree frog nodded and wiped her brow. "Frogs in the trees spotted her earlier," she said. "Some left, but we decided to keep working." Tubs hopped beside the yellow tree frog through the cattail forest, and together they called out Lila's name.

Soon they came upon a line of frogs, and behind that another. Behind the frogs, Tubs could see Virgil and the water rats, covered in mud up to their knees. They had tied ropes to trunks of trees, creating a pulley. They were working hard to haul a massive stone into the mouth of the pipe while a group of crawfish steadied it from the sides. The song of the frogs was nearly deafening, and it was joined by the high-pitched whine of a siren.

Everywhere Tubs looked he could see frogs

surrounding the pipe, creating a ring around the water rats, protecting them from every side. Around that ring of frogs there was another ring of frogs, and around that another. They drifted in the water, some of them already covered in the dark goo. They stood on top of the pipe and on the shore and in the shallows, and in the distance, he could see them standing on the wall that looked out onto the factory.

"We're here in case anyone tries to stop them," said the yellow tree frog. "Or slow them down." She opened her pack and handed a rock to each frog she passed. "If Pythia comes, she'll have to get through us first."

"She could eat us," said Tubs.

"She could," said the yellow tree frog. "But that pipe is more dangerous than a hungry alligator."

These are the bravest creatures I've ever known, thought Tubs. He took a rock and went to stand beside them.

The terrible goo lapped against the stone pushing it back, and the water rats pulled with all their might on the ropes to bring it closer to the mouth of the pipe. Just when it seemed the stone was nearly in place and they could hear it clank against metal, one of the rats slipped in the mud and the stone fell back. The crawfish caught it and brought it forward—though they were covered with the goo and some of them were unable to see.

Suddenly there was a warning cry from the frogs who were guarding the crawfish. Tubs turned just in time to see a ripple on the surface of the swamp. Soon the ripple became a wave and it began to crest. The frogs in the water locked arms, and the frogs on the shore rushed to help them, rocks in hand, but there was little they could do.

Pythia rose from the swamp, her eyes glinting and her jaws fixed in a terrifying grin. She was right,

Tubs thought. I stayed in the swamp and now there is nothing but misery.

The alligator pushed through the crowd of frogs, sending them flailing through the murky water, then turned and fixed her eyes directly on Tubs.

28

Tubs trembled in the water beneath Pythia's stare. His skin itched and burned from the poison that flowed from the pipe. Frogs were still singing as they rushed at the alligator witch, throwing rocks. They climbed atop one another, making a barricade of bodies between Pythia and the water rats. And all along the alarm was still sounding from beyond the factory wall.

There was a loud clang and all the animals turned at once to see. The rats and the crawfish had done

it—they had placed the stone over the mouth of the pipe. But the goo still leaked from around it.

Suddenly Pythia snapped her enormous jaws open and shut. She twisted around, pulling dozens of frogs along with her down into the swirling current. Then she turned and fast as lightning whipped her powerful tail against the stone, smacking it deep into the pipe— sealing it in place. She slid back into the water, leaving bewildered and frightened frogs in her wake.

The crawfish climbed out of the murky shallows, and the water rats sat weary in the mud, nodding to one another with a gruff sort of pride. Virgil lit his pipe and leaned back on his elbows. "Y'all see that alligator witch?" he said.

A cheer rose up and down the embankment as the creatures of the swamp learned the pipe was shut. From somewhere beyond the wall another cheer echoed—as though dozens of voices were calling back to them.

Inside the factory, Lila and Billy had broken the glass case and were trying with all their might to pull the switch when suddenly they saw the pipe bulge and start to crack, and dark goo began oozing from it. Lila hopped on Billy's back and they flew from the room, watching as the ooze flooded the floor beneath them.

The bog lemmings who were still in the factory ran to keep ahead of it, climbing the wall, calling to birds for help. Some were scooped up into the air, and some pushed through cracks and mouseholes to make their escape.

Lila and Billy landed outside in the soft mud near the pipe. They walked together hand in wing toward the water and the sound of singing. And then Lila saw, in the distance, weary frogs pulling broad leaves from the ground to clean their sticky, itchy skin. Standing among them, covered in mud and bumps, grinning from ear to ear, was Tubs.

The hospital was full that evening. Lila bandaged broken claws, stitched cut paws, administered medicines and balms and shots. Though it was crowded, and though creatures had cuts and scrapes and welts, Lila was smiling.

"I'm happy to say everyone will make a full recovery," she told Tubs, handing him another tube of arnica balm. "Even you."

"Even Gloria?" Tubs asked.

"Even Gloria," she said.

"What was it like inside the factory?" he asked her.

"It was smooth and cold and strange," she said. "And then the lemmings came, and it got *really* strange."

Tubs laughed. "Their magic worked."

"Their magic, Roy's hammer, and a very angry

duck," she said. "But they'll have it fixed in a day or two—people are like us, they're hard workers."

"If they don't fix it, we can't break it tomorrow," said Tubs. Lila laughed. She looked so happy now.

"Remember when Billy thought you were a witch?" Tubs said.

"I remember it like it was yesterday," said Lila, "because it *was* yesterday. But you can't blame Billy. It's hard to think straight when you've lost your feathers and don't know why."

29

Tubs left the hospital and walked along the edge of the water. Above him the sky was full of stars spread across the blackness, and the moon was high. He could feel a new song out there waiting to find him. As he walked along the edge of the swamp, Tubs wondered what had made Pythia help them instead of eating them. Then he wondered if maybe she did eat a few of them and no one noticed in all the commotion.

Maybe she helped them because she received a

new prophecy, he thought. Maybe we'll never know. Maybe the swamp called for an idea—and an alligator showed up.

Or maybe the swamp had dreamed them all—frogs and bog lemmings and fearless, featherless ducks, and alligator witches. "Life is mysterious," said Tubs to the stars.

The lights were blazing at Tubs's house by the time he arrived home. Fireflies blinked around the dock like glitter in the air. Small boats were moored outside and every kind of creature sat on the dock or drifted in the water or roosted on the roof.

As he got closer, he could smell a delicious scent wafting over the breeze. Chicory and fiddlehead ferns and porcupine sedge and water plantain.

Inside the house, Beau was cooking, standing at the

stove in his cowboy boots holding a wooden spoon and wearing an apron. The portrait of Elodie seemed to smile even bigger than before.

"Tubs, where you been?" shouted Beau.

The yellow tree frog was pouring glasses of rose-mallow wine and the house was packed with frogs he had known forever and frogs he had never seen before that day. There were frogs at the piano, a frog playing his clarinet. Frogs dancing in the living room. There were frogs looking at maps and drawings of the factory spread out on the kitchen table. There were even frogs who still had tails chasing each other out onto the dock, or sitting in boats looking up at the stars.

"How do all these frogs suddenly know where I live?" Tubs asked.

"Well, our species sure does love a party, huh?" said Beau. "Reckon they couldn't resist."

"It's because everyone loves the new song," said the tree frog. "It's good to change things up every two hundred million years or so."

"Yup," said Virgil. "Everyone likes a good day of house cleaning. Felt real nice to clean up the swamp."

"Everyone likes a good light display," said a firefly. "They must have seen us shining from the other end of the swamp."

"Everyone," said Roy, "is here for the magic! Just look around. Beau has made some magic soup, Lila gave us magic balm, Tubs wrote a magic song, the fireflies made magical sparkling lights. The trees grew magically out of the ground and the birds glided magically into the sky. And our magic eyes in front of our magic brains got to see it all."

"That ain't magic," said Virgil. "That's just how life is. A creature is a creature."

Tubs looked up and saw Lila and Gloria standing

in the doorway. Gloria was wearing her tie. There was a downy covering of blue along her wings where her feathers were starting to grow back. Lila waved and they made their way through the crowd.

Gloria looked weak but happy. "I'm sorry I missed all the excitement," she said. "I like to see a pipe explode as much as the next sparrow."

"How are you feeling?" Tubs asked.

Gloria looked up at her friend with shining black eyes, "Better," she said. "I never spent so much time in my tree before. Really got me thinking. Hey, Tubs," she said. "You know what side of the tree has the most leaves?"

Tubs opened his mouth to answer.

"The outside," said Gloria.

"See?" said Lila. "She's better already."

Billy waddled across the room and gave Lila a peck on the cheek; then he hopped up to stand on top of the piano. He wore a green hat with a flower in the brim, and his remaining feathers were combed back neatly.

Tubs took out his harmonica and someone shouted, "Play that zydeco, Tubs!" The new frogs and the old, and the lemmings and the birds, and the crawfish and the water rats all danced long into the night, the way they had every night for thousands of years.

Around midnight, the frogs broke into "Kiss Me, I'm the Fastest" and began to take their boats home. As the guests began to leave, they called out, "See you at the pipe" to one another, and "Can't wait to break that pipe," and "Get a good rest, now." And "Don't forget your hammer." "Don't forget your ropes. We might need to climb the smokestack this time." "Lila, you got them papers to show the other humans?"

As Virgil was leaving, he gave Tubs a wink and a pat on the arm.

"Just between you and me," said Virgil, "I can't wait to do all this again tomorrow."

When everyone had gone home, Tubs and Lila sat in the red-and-white boat, looking up at the stars. "You're not going to be here tomorrow, are you?" she asked.

"How did you know?" he said.

"Tubs, I've been looking at your face since we were tadpoles."

"I've been thinking about what Pythia said," he told her.

"But you know that prophecy isn't true," she said. "And now that we know the pipe is there and how to break it, creatures will start getting better."

"A lot of the prophecy was true," said Tubs. "I had to leave to find the pipe. Frogs everywhere are singing my song, and I stood beside the greats today while they protected the swamp. But I mean what she said when she was thinkin' 'bout eating me. Pythia said my home was wherever I played songs, and she was right, Lila."

Lila smiled. "Doesn't take an alligator witch to know that about you, Tubs. Music is your home. Just like it was for Elodie."

30

Tubs put on his gold-and-crimson vest and his best shoes and left as the first rays of sunlight spread out over the water. He took his harmonica and his bindle stick, and a jug of rose-mallow wine.

There were no salamanders or star-nosed moles waiting for the train this time. And he hoisted himself into the boxcar and found a place to sit—not too close to the open door, but not too far from it, either. Tubs watched as people bustled on and off the train;

they hugged each other and smiled. A creature is a creature, he thought; they're so much like us.

As the train began to roll, it sang its own song, and he took out his harmonica and played along. Outside, the trees spread their branches to the heavens, and wisps of clouds danced in the blue. The train passed houses and buildings and fields. The grasses and the flowers and the kudzu blurred by. Suddenly through the clearing he could see the swamp, bright and green and shining.

Soon the train was racing, and Tubs felt the wind in his face. He held on tight and watched the whole world speed past.

ACKNOWLEDGMENTS

Thanks to Eli. And thanks to Eli again for the soundtrack of my writing life. Thanks to Anna Stein, Claudia Gabel, Stephanie Guerdan, and Jacquelynn Burke. Thanks to my parents for eagerly awaiting each chapter. Thanks to Em for her genius and magic spells. Thanks to Ann Godwin, always. Thanks to my partner and fellow traveler, Marc Lepson. We did it, ML.